THE WEDDING

SARAH EDGHILL

BLOODHOUND
— B O O K S —

CHAPTER ONE

Meg has been waiting outside the entrance to Hammersmith tube for nearly half an hour. The exhaust fumes are tickling her throat, the noise is making her head pound, and her feet – squeezed into these ridiculously high heels – are throbbing. Every couple of minutes, trains which are arriving hundreds of feet below ground, disgorge fresh waves of commuters who force her to move to one side as they flood up the steps behind her, striding off towards work stations, desks and tills, phones clamped to ears, footsteps clacking along the pavements.

She feels like an idiot, just standing here like this. There's a guy a few feet away, selling copies of *The Big Issue*. She should have bought one when she first got here, but she was expecting to be picked up by the others any minute, so didn't go over to him. Now, too much time has passed and the whole thing feels awkward, so she keeps her head turned the other way.

She checks her watch: less than two minutes have passed since the last time she looked and she's freezing. She stamps her feet on the pavement to keep them warm, but stops again immediately, when the shoes pinch into her heels. This is so irritating: Ali and Nancy are really late now. She tuts and shakes her head – even though there's no one to see.

Meg had been pleased with herself when she arrived at Hammersmith on time, because getting out of the house promptly nowadays – even without a small child clinging to one or both legs – is a monumental achievement. That makes it even more frustrating that the others still aren't here. Meg knows Ali drives a black Audi – a proper career-girl car – but she has given up stepping forward every time she thinks she sees one of those approaching: virtually everyone in Hammersmith seems to be driving a black Audi this morning.

The wind whips up the hem of her dress, exposing her knees, and she grabs the flimsy material, tugging it down again, feeling it tighten across her midriff. A woman in a smart navy suit throws a glance her way as she walks past and Meg feels her cheeks flushing. Why did she ever think she could get away with a dress like this? It's too tight; too revealing. If only she'd managed to lose a bit of weight in time for this weekend.

When the invitation first arrived, back in April, it seemed achievable to drop a dress size, or maybe more. Meg stuck the gold-embossed card onto the front of the fridge with a *CBeebies* magnet and her pulse quickened every time she walked past and glanced at it:

Mrs and Mrs Mark Johnson
request the pleasure of your company at the wedding of their
daughter, Polly Jane, to Adam Harris.

Having this wedding to look forward to has been exciting – it isn't every day one of your best friends gets married. But Meg was also fired up by the fact that having a major event in the diary would be the incentive she needed to shed some of her excess baby weight.

'You must buy yourself something to wear,' Joe had said. 'You deserve it.'

She wasn't sure that was true but knew that, if she could lose a few pounds, she'd feel less guilty about rewarding herself with a new dress. The local gym was an intimidating place with smoked glass floor-to-ceiling windows, behind which it was just possible to see the outlines of lithe figures in Lycra throwing themselves about on running machines and cross trainers. Meg had never been inside, but forced herself to walk in the door and flick through the information leaflet, which was pushed across the reception desk by a teenage girl wearing excessive eye make-up and tight Lycra shorts.

The cost of full membership made Meg gasp, but she was too embarrassed to walk out without signing up for something, so ended up booking an introductory course of aerial hoop classes. Back home, she went online and added vast quantities of salad and fresh fish onto her next Tesco food delivery and started reading up about the benefits of increasing the amount of protein in her diet. As the wedding invitation twinkled at her from the front of the fridge, she realised she really was feeling motivated by the prospect of this new regime: she would prepare healthy meals, work out several times a week, cut back on the wine and in no time at all she'd be a slimmed-down, highly toned size 12 again. Or at least a 14.

But it hasn't quite worked out like that and God knows where the last three months have gone. For a start, she only attended two of those stupid hoop sessions: it turns out that balancing on a flimsy piece of metal in mid-air isn't an ideal form of exercise for someone who suffers from mild vertigo.

The healthy eating plan hasn't gone well either: it has now become such a habit to finish the bits of fishfinger and sausage left on the children's plates, rather than scrape them into the bin, that Meg hardly notices herself doing it anymore. She has been trying to cut out snacks and reduce portion sizes, but it's bloody hard not to eat sugary rubbish when you're tired all the time.

So, the weight stayed on; the wedding date loomed. A couple of weeks ago, in desperation, she tried a new intermittent fasting diet everyone was talking about, where you only drink water or herbal tea for sixteen hours a day: one of the mums at nursery said she'd lost 5lbs in a week. Meg lasted three days, feeling constantly nauseous, snapping at the kids for no reason and struggling to sleep at night. She lost just 1lb. Too little, too late, as her mother would say.

A horn blares beside her, making her jump, then a car door opens, so close it nearly scrapes her shin.

'Get in!' Ali is yelling. 'Quickly! There's a bus right behind me.'

Meg tumbles into the back seat, dragging her case after her and gathering in the flimsy folds of her dress as she pulls the door shut.

'Bloody hell, this is a nightmare place to stop!' Ali turns to look back over her shoulder at the traffic as she signals to pull out. 'Whose idea was it to pick you up here?'

'Well... I think it was yours?' Meg is trying to reach behind her for the seatbelt, but can't move her right arm beneath the case, so the car's sensor begins to ping.

'Shove that on the floor.' Nancy stretches out her arm from the front passenger seat and tries to help Meg manoeuvre the case into the footwell. 'Bloody hell, Meg, it weighs a ton! What have you got in here – gold bullion?'

'No! Just a few bits and pieces. It's hard knowing what to pack for something like this. I've got a change of clothes for tomorrow and I thought it would be cold in the evening...'

But the other two aren't listening. Nancy has now turned

back to face the front and Ali is swearing at a black cab, which is cutting in front of the Audi.

It takes several minutes for them to negotiate their way around the Hammersmith one-way system, with drivers leaning on their horns on all sides. Meg tries not to make it obvious that the fingers of her left hand are clenched tightly around the door handle, and she only feels her shoulders drop again when Ali accelerates up the flyover and they head out of town.

'So, how are you both?' she asks. 'Thank you so much for driving, Ali, I really appreciate it.'

'Not a problem.' Ali lifts her head and grins at her in the rear-view mirror. 'Sorry, haven't even said a proper hello, but it's great to see you, Meg. Were you waiting there long?'

'Hardly any time at all,' Meg lies.

'The traffic has been awful,' Ali continues. 'I left home at seven, and should have been at Nancy's in forty minutes, but it took over an hour, then there was an accident on Wandsworth Bridge so they sent us all round the houses. Those twenty mile an hour speed zones they've introduced everywhere don't help either – and if you're not sitting in queues, you're trying to avoid bloody cyclists, who think they own the roads!'

'That's south London for you,' says Nancy.

'And north London, and *west* London.' Ali laughs, her deep guttural cackle so familiar, that, even with her eyes closed, Meg could pick her out in a crowd.

Now they're finally on the road, her pulse is racing again – in a good way. Despite the ongoing trauma of the last few weeks – the dieting, the struggle to find a dress to wear and the worry about getting everything organised at home – she has been so looking forward to Polly and Adam's wedding; energised at the prospect of seeing her old friends and spending twenty-four precious hours away from the humdrum of East Finchley.

Last night, she realised this will be the first time she's been away on her own since Ollie was born, which is crazy.

Before Meg had babies, she always swore she wouldn't turn into one of those mothers who sacrifice their own lives when they start a family. Not that it has felt like any kind of sacrifice, but somehow the weeks turned into months, then into years, and there was never any reason for her to go away overnight on her own. Not that she has ever particularly wanted to: she loves being at home with the children; the little terraced house in north London is her happy place. But it's funny how staying put seems to have turned into a long-term habit. Anyway, here she is, finally escaping for a night away, after five years.

Ali is describing a work trip she tried to make the other week, when a car in front of her broke down in the Rotherhithe Tunnel and a journey that should have taken twenty minutes, took four hours. 'I was stuck in solid traffic, desperate for a wee!' she's saying. 'The recovery truck had to reverse in from the other end of the tunnel. The guy in the delivery van behind me was so stressed he was beating his hands on the steering wheel. I thought he was going to have a heart attack!'

Meg watches her friend flick on the indicator, pulling smoothly into the outside lane as she finishes the story. Ali is such a good driver, effortlessly concentrating on the road and talking at the same time. This is more than Meg herself can manage: two days ago, she nearly knocked down some woman on a zebra crossing, when Tallulah spilt water over herself and started screaming in the back seat of the car.

'You've got the patience of a saint, Al,' Nancy is saying. 'I think I would have had a major hissy fit.'

'How are things with you, Nancy?' Meg asks.

'Oh, the same old shit.' Nancy laughs. 'Thank God we've just had a couple of weeks off for Christmas, I've never needed the holidays so much.'

'Why was last term worse than usual?' asks Ali.

'It wasn't, not really. I've got a couple of little buggers in this year group though. Can't wait to hand them over, and the Christmas term is always long and stressful.'

'You're a hero,' Ali laughs. 'Parents across south London salute you.'

'Yeah, right,' Nancy says. 'They're clearly not the ones who come storming into my classroom to demand I stop giving out detentions and start re-grading the appalling homework handed in late by their rude kids!'

'You must enjoy it, though, really?' Meg asks. 'I mean, it's such a worthwhile thing to be doing.' Even as the words come out of her mouth, she hears how trite they sound. As usual, she's trying too hard.

'It's just a bloody job,' Nancy says. 'Some days it's mostly about crowd control, never mind teaching them stuff that will help them achieve anything in life. I might as well have become a probation officer.'

Meg is sure she doesn't mean that – although she also has no doubt Nancy would do a great job of controlling hardened criminals in Belmarsh. Meg could never admit it to anyone, but she has always felt slightly intimidated by this friend of hers, who was so forceful, opinionated and brimming with self-confidence when they all met at Leeds University.

Eleven years later, Nancy is an equally forceful, opinionated, self-confident teacher at a rough secondary school in Balham. Meg doesn't envy the kids in her class who are on the receiving end of her sarcasm – and she can't imagine Nancy suffers foolish parents gladly either.

Meg herself is having to deal with teachers for the first time, now that Ollie has started school and, as someone who has always been deferential by nature and slightly scared of

SARAH EDGHILL

authority, she can't imagine being anything other than polite and respectful to Ollie's teacher, Miss Carmody.

But the dealings they've had over the last few months have frequently been awkward, and Meg sometimes wishes she had some of Nancy's hard-nosed attitude to life: it must be great to not give a shit what anyone thinks about you or your child.

'Are the kids really that bad?' Ali is asking. 'I mean, they're still young – what, thirteen or fourteen? Surely, it's mostly about raging hormones at that age, rather than criminal tendencies?'

'Yes, but raging hormones can cause chaos,' says Nancy. 'And when you're dealing with more than thirty separate sets of raging hormones, every day brings a fresh set of flash points, so you need to come down hard on some of them. It's the well-behaved ones you feel sorry for. They work hard and keep their heads down, but because you're dealing with the kids who are kicking off, it sometimes seems like the others get forgotten in the chaos.'

They have now left behind the tower blocks and industrial estates of west London, and the road widens into three lanes as it turns into the motorway. Meg stares out of the window at the trees whipping past, litter clinging to branches behind streaks of grey crash-barriers.

Will Ollie and Tallulah turn into out-of-control, hormonal teenagers? It seems impossible to imagine them ever being that old: at five and two, they are still biddable, loving, happy little human beings. Well, Tallulah is, anyway. Meg can't imagine herself as a mother to older children who slam doors and sulk and spend all day staring at a phone screen. Although maybe nowadays that sort of thing happens even before they reach their teens; one of the other five-year-olds in Ollie's Reception class has his own mobile and, outside the school gates, Meg and her fellow parents frequently share appalled looks and shocked conversations about it. There's no way she'll be letting her kids have phones for a very long time.

'Anyway,' Nancy is saying. 'There's always a bit of jostling for position that goes on, kids asserting themselves. It's amazing how moving up a year suddenly makes even the timid ones more bolshy. But let's not bang on about school and my bloody job, it's dull, dull, dull. I've got the day off! Let's enjoy being away from it all.'

A coach pulls out in front of the Audi without signalling and Ali swears under her breath as she slams on the brakes, then moves into the fast lane to overtake it.

Meg jumps as her phone begins to ring. As she sees Joe's name flashing up on the screen, she's already panicking. She has only been gone for a couple of hours but that's long enough for all kinds of bedlam to have kicked off at home. Joe is usually long gone by this time in the morning, joining the millions of commuters trudging towards tube stations and travelling into central London. He doesn't know what it's like in their kitchen on a weekday morning, and has never seen the tantrums or heard the yelling; he has no idea that one tiny thing can spark a meltdown in one or both children. She imagines breakfast plates upended on the kitchen floor; Ollie sticking his fingers into the blue flame of the gas ring on the hob; Tallulah slipping and bashing her head as she tries to clamber up onto the kitchen table.

Meg's finger shakes as she swipes to take the call. 'What's happened? Are the kids okay? What's wrong?' She can't control the panic in her voice.

'Nothing, they're fine.' Joe sounds tinny and disconnected, but she can hear shrieking in the background, thumps as if a door is being kicked. 'But Ollie can't find his pencil case – you know, the dinosaur one with the felt tips in? He says he can't go to school without it.'

Her shoulders drop a little; at least no one's on the way to A&E. But this still isn't a minor problem, she knows how angry Ollie gets when things don't quite go to plan.

'Well, it was in his room, last night. Have you tried looking under his bed, or on the windowsill? Or, maybe it's in his book bag already? We might have left it in the bathroom, Ollie was in there with me earlier, when I was brushing my teeth.' Meg is aware of a sound coming from the seat in front of her. It's Nancy. She can't tell if she's snorting or stifling a laugh, but Meg immediately tenses again. 'Look, Joe, if you can't find it, he'll just have to go in without it. Miss Carmody won't mind; she knows I'm going away. But why are you only just looking for that now? It's getting on for nine o'clock – the kids are going to be so late!'

Nancy might just be reacting to something she's reading on her phone, but Meg is sure she's listening to this one-sided conversation. She doesn't need to see her friend's face to know she is rolling her eyes at the domestic disarray she can hear being acted out in front of her.

For the last two hours, Meg has been trying to quell a rolling undercurrent of guilt about not being at home this morning to get the kids ready. What if Joe – competent, calm Joe – can't cope? Deep down, she knows he can, but in the run-up to this wedding she has been feeling increasingly guilty about leaving him to deal with everything – even though he insists it will all be fine and he's more than capable of looking after his own children for the weekend. If Meg is honest, she knows this is more about her than him; no one else has ever been in sole charge of Ollie and Tallulah overnight – even their own father – so she's finding it ridiculously hard to let go. Had she started taking some time away when the children were younger, she would have overcome all these doubts and fears and got used to the fact that she is *not* the only one able to look after her own kids. But as more time has passed, she has become increasingly unwilling – or unable – to face leaving Joe alone to deal with everything. Now, unfortunately, this conversation is confirming her worst fears.

The smallness of it is also making her embarrassed in front of these old friends who have known her for so many years – since way before she became a wife and a mother and stopped being the Meg they knew when they all met, eleven years ago. This is the sort of conversation that must take place between parents on a regular basis but, as she sits in the back seat of this smart Audi, she feels a prickle of mortification. She is seeing herself through her friends' eyes and doesn't like it. Ali and Nancy don't have children; they have stressful careers and busy social lives and their priorities are very different to her own. Neither of them will understand why a missing dinosaur pencil case is something to get worked up about.

Poor Joe, who will have no idea about any of this and only called to ask her a simple question, bears the brunt of Meg's embarrassment as it turns to irritation. 'Look, you'll just have to sort it!' she snaps. 'I can't do anything right now... Well, it's not my problem if you're going to be late for work! No, I'm sorry, Joe, I'm not getting cross, it's just...'

She doesn't want to be having this conversation with her husband. What she wants to be saying is, *Joe, I hope you're coping without me. I'm nervous about going to this wedding and I think I look bloody awful and I wish you were here beside me so you could give me a hug and make everything all right again.* But, instead, she is getting irritated and jumping down his throat and, not surprisingly, can hear the hurt in his voice.

Ali half-turns her head when Meg ends the call. 'Typical man!' she says. 'I bet you left everything prepared and sorted for him, didn't you? But he still can't cope!'

'He's actually really good with the kids.' Meg knows Ali is

joking, but still leaps to Joe's defence. 'He's just rushed, that's all. He's got to drop Tallulah at nursery before he gets Ollie to school and that's going to make him really late for work. It's always manic in the mornings and Ollie can get a bit hyper and naughty, especially when things don't go to plan. I know it doesn't sound like a big deal, but Joe isn't used to juggling it all.'

'Although, of course, *you* manage it,' points out Ali. 'Every single day.'

Meg nods and smiles. 'Guess I do.' Ali isn't knocking Joe; Ali loves Joe – all her friends do – she's just being supportive.

'What you should have done, is walk out of the house having prepared nothing at all and made no plans, leaving him to deal with the entire shit show,' Nancy says. 'It's the only way men will ever learn to fend for themselves. It's all too easy for them to leave everything to the woman because she's invariably the one who's organised and efficient and just gets on and does it all. I bet you got all the kids' school stuff ready. You probably even ironed Joe's shirt!'

'I did *not*.' Meg crosses her arms and stares out of the side window again. She not only ironed Joe's shirt – late last night after she finished putting the children to bed, tidying the house and making supper – she also put together the packed lunches for the following day, cooked a lasagna for the three of them to have in her absence, sorted Ollie's book bag, filled Tallulah's nursery backpack with wipes and a change of clothes – the potty training isn't going well – and laid out Ollie's uniform and Tallulah's clothes, ready for this morning. At the last minute she also made a couple of pleading phone calls to fellow parents and arranged for both children to have play dates after school and nursery this afternoon, so Joe won't have to leave work early to pick them up.

There's no way she is going to admit any of this to Nancy,

because she knows what kind of reaction she'll get. It's strange that someone who has chosen education as a career, seems to have such little time or empathy for children and the parents who have to look after them. Or maybe, she thinks, it's just that Nancy doesn't have any empathy for her and her children.

'I've really been looking forward to today,' Meg says brightly, determined to change the subject. 'Do you realise, this is the first time all four of us will have been together, since *my* wedding!'

'No! Really?' Ali shakes her head. 'That's insane – how long ago was that? Five years?'

'Nearly seven.'

'Are you sure?' Nancy leans sideways and looks back through the gap in the front seats. 'Weren't we all at Polly and Adam's engagement party last year, when she wore that amazing orange dress?'

'I wasn't there,' says Meg. 'Ollie had chicken pox.'

'Or, what about your birthday, a couple of years ago, Al,' Nancy says. 'When we went to that rooftop bar in Covent Garden?'

'I was on holiday,' says Meg. 'I've been working it out – it was definitely my wedding, the last time we were all together.'

'Wow,' says Nancy. 'Where does the time go?'

Meg had been twenty-two when she and Joe got married. At the time, she hadn't felt particularly young, but she was aware her university friends were on a different life trajectory and nowhere near the stage where they were ready to settle down. When she announced she was pregnant, just four months after the wedding, she sensed some judgement – particularly from Nancy. 'Are you really going to give up work?' she'd asked, sounding appalled. 'You've hardly got started?'

'I'm not like you, Nance,' Meg had said, her body brimming

with hormones, her heart so full of love for Joe that she couldn't imagine ever feeling happier. 'I don't have a proper career; it doesn't matter if I stop working. The world of recruitment won't come crashing down without my social media skills. There are hundreds of thousands of people who can do what I've been doing.'

But she understood her choice wouldn't have suited the others: all three of them so bright and driven, so dedicated to their professions. Ali, one of only a handful of women who studied engineering at Leeds, always had *career woman* written all over her, like words stamped through a stick of rock. She is now a mechanical engineer, whose work regularly takes her to exotic locations, from Dubai and Singapore to South America and the Caribbean. She talks about it dismissively, as if international travel is a bore. For Meg, whose world now rarely extends beyond the shops, cafés and playgroups of East Finchley, it sounds unbelievably exciting.

Nancy probably wouldn't describe herself as high powered, but she is wedded to her career and, for all her professed dislike of young people, she appears to be carving out a reputation for herself in teaching. She studied philosophy at Leeds, and seemed to hate every second of it. 'What good is a philosophy degree?' she used to rant. 'What use is all this bloody theorising when the world is going to hell in a handcart and mankind is causing catastrophic climate change that will destroy the planet before future generations get the chance to ruin it for themselves?'

They'd all expected Nancy to go into some form of political activism, but she slid effortlessly into education and, at just twenty-seven, was made a head of year. Nearly three years later, she is now also head of the English department at the Balham school which she constantly slags off, but clearly loves.

And then, of course, there's Polly. Fun, bubbly, caring Polly, who was such a pivotal part of their friendship group at university, and who is now gathering them all together again for her wedding. Meg studied English alongside Polly, but her own mediocre degree didn't compare to Polly's first-class honours, which catapulted her into a consultancy job. Joe says the company Polly works for is one of the best in the country, but Meg doesn't even really understand what consultants do.

When she lets herself think about the way their lives have progressed, Meg feels rather small beside her friends. So, she doesn't let herself think about it very often. Anyway, she loves her life and adores her family, and isn't motherhood the most important job in the world? Despite their differences, their friendship is stronger than ever – that's what she always tells Joe: the friends you make when you're a student, will be friends for life. She almost believes it, even though she doesn't see as much of the other three women any more, and there can be no denying that their disparate lives have led to an almost imperceptible drifting apart.

'This weekend is going to be great,' Nancy is saying. 'If anyone is going to do a wedding in style, it will be Polly.'

'She'll look stunning,' Ali agrees.

'And isn't it fantastic,' Meg says. 'All of us being together again?'

'I was thinking about that, the other day,' Ali says. 'In some ways, it seems like no time at all since we were at Leeds. Back then, we thought we were really grown up. But we were just playing at it. We had no worries, no ties, no idea what life held in store.'

'And look at us now,' says Nancy.

'Proper, responsible human beings,' grins Meg.

'With proper, responsible jobs,' adds Nancy.

'And proper, responsible mortgages and tax bills and all that other grown-up crap,' says Ali. 'Who'd have thought it?'

'I love you guys!' Meg says.

Later, she will remember that conversation and wonder how so much shared history can have started to mean so little, in just twenty-four hours.

CHAPTER TWO

The last hour of the journey is stressful. When they come off the motorway, the digital display on the Audi's satnav informs them there are only twenty-three miles to their destination and the journey will take thirty-seven minutes. 'We'll be there in time,' Ali says.

But within minutes of leaving the motorway, they find themselves driving along country lanes which seem to get narrower and more overgrown with every passing mile. At one point, a tractor pulls out of a field in front of them and rattles agonisingly slowly along the single-track road for what seems like hours, although it's probably only a few minutes. When it eventually turns into a farmyard, they all cheer; Ali puts her foot on the accelerator, and they're pushed back into their seats as the car picks up speed.

Meg's stomach rumbles loudly and she pushes her hands onto it in a vain attempt to stop the noise. She had breakfast with Tallulah at 5.30am, then bought a flapjack in the corner shop to eat during the tube journey to Hammersmith. She'd been hoping they might stop at a services on the M4, but neither of the others suggested it.

She hasn't had a chance to look at either of them properly this morning, but from back here, they both seem as skinny as ever. There was never anything of Ali at uni: Meg sometimes wondered if she had an eating disorder, but there weren't any obvious signs and Polly used to say Ali just had a crazily fast metabolism.

Nancy was slim as well, but with an athlete's figure: strong shoulders, taut stomach and toned legs. She played in the uni hockey team and went out on her bike at the crack of dawn. She was obsessive about healthy eating and they used to joke that eating a meal with her was like socialising with the food police. Meg remembers standing in a takeaway one evening, squirting mayonnaise onto a pile of greasy chips while Nancy looked on and shook her head: 'Frying carbs at high temperatures creates dangerous chemicals, Meg,' she'd said. 'You need to make better decisions about what you put into your body.'

Whoever had been there with them – Meg can't now remember who it was – had screamed with laughter and started waving a chip in Nancy's face, but Meg had felt cowed. As they walked back along the pavement, she ate the chips, but didn't enjoy them; she'd been cross with herself for not being able to let the comment wash over her.

Right now, she would kill for a bag of greasy chips. 'Anyone else hungry?' she asks, but Ali shakes her head and Nancy doesn't answer. Her head is bent over her phone screen, her finger swiping so fast that Meg wonders how her brain has time to register what she's seeing.

She stares out of the window and sighs: who knows when they'll next eat? That's something Meg dreads about weddings: the guests never know how long it will be until the formalities have been dealt with – photographs, meet and greet, initial mingling. All the hanging around doesn't bother the bride and groom, because they're at the centre of it and too busy to worry about how long it's all taking, but for the guests, it could be hours before they get offered so much as a bite-sized canapé. In the meantime, they'll be standing around in uncomfortable shoes, making polite conversation with people they hardly know and knocking back champagne on an empty stomach.

Speaking of uncomfortable shoes: Meg's are killing her. She has had these blue stilettos for years now – she got them when she graduated from Leeds, part-treat, part-attempt to do something a bit different and stand out from all the other graduates in their hired black gowns and mortar boards. Back then, she managed to wear the stilettos without getting blistered heels or falling over, but for the last few years they've sat in a box at the back of the wardrobe – nowadays she hardly goes out in anything except trainers – and her feet seem to have spread. She's wearing tights, but the skin on her right heel is catching particularly painfully against the hard edge of the shoe and the little toe on her other foot is numb. Desperate to rub her heel, she slides off one of the shoes, knowing as she does so that it's a mistake, because she'll have a job to get the damn thing on again.

Coming around a corner, Ali is forced to slam on the brakes when they see the road ahead is blocked by cows. The animals are being herded out of a barn onto the lane and lumbering along it for a few metres to where a farmer leans against the gate of a field, looking as if he has all the time in the world to oversee the process. Which he probably does.

'Fuck!' Ali jabs frantically at the screen of the satnav. 'Shall we try to find another way round?'

'We'd have to back up for miles,' Nancy points out.

'Let's wait,' Meg suggests. 'There can't be that many of them.'

There are dozens. They can't see into the barn, but black and white beasts trundle out of it in a steady procession and move laboriously slowly down the lane, as the minutes tick by on the Audi's dashboard clock.

'I wonder who else will be going?' Ali asks, as they watch the cows. 'Do you remember that guy Jim, who did English with Polly?'

'I remember him,' Meg says. 'I did English too!'

'And his friend, Toby?'

'God, I loved that boy,' says Nancy. 'Beyond handsome. Looked like Ryan Reynolds.'

'Yes! Do you think he'll be there?'

'No idea, but I know the girls who shared a flat with me in the second year are coming – Sal and Chloe. Remember them?'

'Sort of.' Meg has no idea who Sal and Chloe are.

'How about those twins who did drama – Luke and Daniel?' Nancy says.

Ali shrugs. 'Their names ring a bell, but I can't picture them. What did they look like?'

Meg can't speak, her heart is suddenly in her mouth, her pulse is racing. She can picture Luke very clearly indeed.

'Tall, dark hair, one of them played in the uni football team, but I can't remember which one,' Nancy is saying. 'They were the first set of identical twins I'd ever met. I was fascinated by them – could never tell them apart.'

Ali laughs. 'Can you imagine going out with an identical twin? The way they could mess with your head.'

Meg wants to say something, but her mouth is dry, her mind working fast but somehow not coming up with a sensible comment.

She smooths the material of her dress, pulling it down across her legs. As she does so, her finger slides across a ladder in her tights, just behind one knee. Shit! It's only small but it's bound to run. If she was at home, she could paint on some clear nail varnish to stop it getting any bigger, but she didn't bring anything like that in her washbag. Maybe one of the others will have some. She puts her finger on the ladder again and feels it widen.

Bloody typical. How did she do that? She has always been clumsy. Friends at Leeds used to laugh about 'Meg' catastrophes. 'Do you remember when she tripped on a bathmat in your flat and nearly pulled the basin away from the wall!' Nancy would say. 'Or that time when she was pissed in McDonalds and dropped her phone down the loo?'

Meg would smile and laugh along with them, pretending she didn't mind playing the fool and that it didn't hurt.

Ollie is clumsy too and she and Joe are frequently telling him off for breaking things and not concentrating on what he's doing. Although, over the last year or so, she has begun to think it's not just clumsiness: her son can be wilful at times and has always had a temper. He broke one of Tallulah's dolls last weekend, Meg was standing in the kitchen and turned round just as Ollie pulled the plastic arm backwards until it snapped off. He looked up and saw her watching him, but his expression didn't change; there was no remorse, no shame. Flustered, Meg had grabbed the doll and hidden it at the bottom of the kitchen bin; she told herself that she didn't want Tallulah to see and get upset, but she realised she was also hiding the broken toy from Joe.

A couple of days later, she was taking the bin bag outside and saw the outline of the broken doll at the bottom. By that time, the whole thing didn't seem so dramatic. She wondered then – and wonders again now – whether she has been overthinking the whole thing? All these little incidents that keep happening – it probably *is* just clumsiness, which means the whole thing is genetic, and her boy is just taking after his cack-handed mother! Funnily enough, it has never occurred to her before: that this might be her fault. Poor Ollie.

'Joe will have dropped the kids off, ages ago,' she says. 'I hope he managed to find that pencil case.'

Neither of the others answer. Ali is leaning forward, glaring at the cows and tapping her fingers on the steering wheel. Nancy is still doing something on her phone.

It was silly to let herself start thinking about Ollie; it's making her feel as if there's a giant fist around her heart and it's squeezing so tightly, she can hardly breathe. She really misses her babies, and it's such a big deal to be here, on her own. Although she has often said she wishes she could have some time to herself, now she's having exactly that, it seems all wrong. Knowing Ollie and Tallulah are more than a hundred miles away makes her feel fragmented and vulnerable, as if a part of her own body has been ripped off.

'He gets a bit worked up about things,' she says. 'Ollie, I mean. He's only five, so it's something he's bound to grow out of. But he isn't finding school easy. Or rather, they aren't finding him easy!' She laughs, to show this isn't a serious conversation.

Ali glances back at her and smiles, but Meg can tell she isn't really listening.

'I think most children go through stages where they play up, don't they?' she continues. 'It's just hard when it's your child. I feel like I'm constantly on the back foot, making excuses for him and apologising to other parents. I mean, I think it's quite normal, the naughtiness, but we're not really sure how to deal with it, and his teacher – God, that woman hates me!'

'Poor you,' says Ali, absently. 'For fuck's sake, this is so annoying! I've never seen so many bloody cows. Why did they have to move them just when we needed to get by?'

Nearly ten minutes have passed by the time the last cow sways into the second field and the farmer waves at them cheerfully as he swings shut the gate.

'Good call, Meg,' says Nancy.

'How is that my fault?'

'We should have turned around and found a different route.'

'That's all very well to say now, after the event.'

'Shut up, both of you,' Ali said, as she accelerates past the farmer, clods of dried mud spinning up behind the car. Meg looks back through the rear window and sees him standing in the road, hands on hips, glaring at them.

By the time they reach the outskirts of the village where the wedding is being held, they're so stressed they've stopped talking; Ali's knuckles are white as she clutches the steering wheel. Meg's heart is pounding in her chest as she peers through the gap in the front seats, watching the clock on the dashboard move inexorably towards the time when Polly will arrive at the church. She feels sick; she hates being late for anything. She takes some deep breaths, making herself practise the breathing techniques she learnt when she took Tallulah to baby yoga, telling herself that none of this is a problem, it will all be fine.

The digital display clicks onto 12:00 just as they turn a corner and see a line of neatly trimmed yews, marking the edge of the churchyard.

'Thank God,' mutters Ali. 'But there's nowhere to park – look at this place! Shit, what a nightmare.'

'Down there.' Nancy points towards a lane on the right. 'Look, there's a space further along.'

'It's too small!'

'You'll have to try, there's nowhere else. I've never seen so many cars.'

Nancy gets out and guides Ali backwards and forwards into the space between a couple of badly parked four-wheel drives. Two minutes later, as the three of them run back up the lane towards the church, Meg's foot slips out of her shoe and she stops, breathing heavily. There is blood smeared across her heel where the skin has been ripped away beneath the tights. She crams her foot back into the stiletto, wincing with pain as she hobbles up the lane. By the time she catches up with the others, Polly is climbing out of a white Rolls Royce which has pulled up outside the lychgate.

'Wow!' Ali is saying. 'What a fantastic dress!'

'You look *so* beautiful.' Nancy throws her arms around Polly and Meg stands watching them hug, noticing the graceful curve of Polly's tanned forearm wrapped around Nancy's shoulders, the sequinned band of white fabric across her chest.

'Am I officially late now?' Polly is laughing. 'Dad was trying to get me downstairs and out to the car for at least ten minutes, but I was determined not to get here on time. Bride's prerogative.'

'Yes, you're late!' Her father, standing behind her, doesn't look nearly as relaxed. 'Some traditions aren't meant to be upheld. Come on, let's get you inside.'

A bridesmaid dressed in lilac is now getting out of the car and, as she turns towards them, Meg sees it's Polly's sister. She met her a couple of times, years ago when Connie came up to visit Polly at Leeds, but even if she hadn't, there would be no mistaking her for anyone else: the two women have the same snub nose, the same wide grin, the same straw-blonde hair. Connie is younger and slightly taller, but Meg has always thought Polly is prettier.

'Ladies!' An usher is standing on the other side of the gate. 'Can I ask you to go and find a seat, so we can get the bride up to the church?'

'Yes, of course! Come on.' Ali grabs Meg's hand and pulls her up the path. 'Nancy! Put that bride down! Let's go.'

Meg looks back over her shoulder as she is dragged away. She wants to hug Polly as well, desperate not to be left out of this moment. She presumes that all the other guests are sitting patiently inside the church, from where they can hear the organ thundering away. But the three of them are out here together, briefly but fortuitously, and it feels like they have special access to Polly on her big day; only her closest friends are here to see her arrive at the church in a flurry of white silk and red and gold flowers, stepping out of one life and towards another. Only the three of them have the chance to grab these last few precious seconds with their special friend and wish her well before the official ceremony begins.

'Polly!' Meg calls back. 'Hey, you look fabulous!'

But Polly has turned away and is looking down at her sister, who is kneeling to adjust the hem of her dress.

CHAPTER THREE

'**B**ride or groom?' asks another usher, signalling to a pew on the left when Nancy answers. They slide into the empty seats, shuffling along as a protracted, juddering chord bursts from the organ. Meg is first into the pew, so she is stuck against the wall and has to lean forward to catch a glimpse of Polly as she enters the church holding her father's arm and starts to walk down the aisle. Her hair is piled into a bun on the top of her head with pearls woven through some of the strands. She looks relaxed and pretty – oh so pretty – and Meg's eyes fill with tears.

Beside her Ali whispers, 'Isn't she gorgeous?' Then the bride and her father and sister have moved forward and Meg is forced to bend to one side, peering over besuited shoulders and through gaps between outsized hats, towards the altar at the front. She can just about see the back of Polly's head, then catches a glimpse of Adam in a grey morning suit, standing beside her. She has seen photographs of this man, but he's even more handsome in the flesh.

'I can't believe you haven't met Adam yet!' Ali whispers, as if reading her mind. 'He and Polly have been together for ages.'

'It's not as if we haven't tried!' Meg whispers back, hearing defensiveness creep into her voice. 'We kept making plans for a night out, but one time Ollie was sick and I had to cancel last minute. Then, when we set another date, Polly had to work late for a client. Anyway, I've seen Polly on her own. It's not as if we haven't been in touch.'

'Life just gets in the way sometimes, doesn't it,' whispers Ali. 'I live two miles from my old schoolfriend, Nell, and we hardly ever see each other.'

Meg nods, gratefully: it does feel a bit strange, but surely it isn't so unusual that she hasn't yet met the fiancé of one of her closest friends? They're all busy, juggling work and home commitments. And London is such a big place: despite the fact that they all live in the same city, there's actually no reason why their lives should intersect.

Up at the far end of the church, Meg briefly catches sight of Connie as she takes Polly's bouquet and moves backwards to stand in one of the pews.

'Time goes by too fast,' she whispers to Ali. 'I can't believe Tallulah is nearly two. I've kept up with Polly and Adam on socials – she posts a lot about their holidays. They went to that hotel in Malta at Easter. And they keep posting stuff about Adam's dog. He has a cute little ginger spaniel. Have you seen it?'

'I've looked after it!' Nancy says, leaning across. 'I had it for the weekend a few months ago, when Pol and Adam went to Berlin.'

Meg doesn't remember a Berlin trip; she must have missed those posts.

The organ stops as quickly as it started and, in the sudden hush, the congregation stand in silence, waiting for the vicar to speak. Meg's stomach rumbles again and she sucks it in so hard her abs ache. Why is she hungry all the time? It seems unfair that her body needs constant refuelling, while other people can go without food for hours and run marathons on half a Ryvita.

The church is packed. There are bound to be plenty of people here Meg knows, but at the moment she doesn't recognise anyone. She leans to one side to try to get a better view, but there are too many extravagant hats in the way. She would give anything to be a few centimetres taller; even wearing these ridiculously high heels, she still isn't as tall as Nancy or Ali.

'Please be seated!' The vicar's voice booms around the church and there is a shuffling and scraping as people sit back down and retrieve their Order of Service. A man towards the front is coughing and somewhere on the other side of the church, a baby is grizzling.

Her ears still ringing from the thundering chords of the wedding march, Meg tries to think back to the last time she saw Polly: it has been several months. They talk about meeting up, just the two of them, but it never seems to happen. It's not as if they haven't been in touch – they exchange fairly regular texts and Polly occasionally likes Meg's Insta posts about the kids – but the last time they actually got together was a while ago.

They'd met for coffee at a Starbucks near Polly's office; it was before Tallulah started nursery and Meg had taken her into central London on the tube, getting the wheels of the buggy caught on the rim of the train door and having to wait for a kind stranger to help her carry it up the steps at the other end. Polly had been distracted, checking her phone every couple of minutes because she was waiting for a call from a client, and she'd had to leave before Meg was halfway through her frothy, sugary latte.

Tallulah had slept through the entire thing, which had been useful in that it meant the two women could chat uninterrupted, but afterwards Meg felt disappointed. As the important call came in, Polly gave her a hug then dashed away, without so much as a glance at the sleeping toddler. Ever since they sat down, Meg had been automatically pushing the buggy backwards and forwards with one hand, casting occasional glances down at her child, hoping and expecting that at some stage Polly would lean forward and bring the conversation around to her: mention how good she was and ask about their routine at home. Maybe admire Tallulah's cute blonde curls or brush her soft cheek with the tip of her forefinger. But there was nothing.

Now Meg thinks about it, when she had that coffee with Polly, Ollie had only just started doing full days in Reception, which means it was the end of September. How was it possible for so much time to have slipped by?

The vicar announces the number of a hymn, and they all dutifully get to their feet and look down at the words in their Order of Service. Meg glances at her watch: it's lunchtime at school now. Ollie will be sitting at one of the miniature tables in the hall, working his way through the food she packed into his lunchbox. He got sent out of lunch a couple of days ago, she's not entirely sure why – something to do with throwing his carton of juice around. *Please let him behave today, when I'm so far away.*

She'd wanted to talk about all this with Ali and Nancy in the car earlier. She desperately wanted them to hear how tough it has been since Ollie started school and how small and vulnerable she has felt. Not that either of her friends would have been able to relate to it. What do they know about having to deal with the mummy mafia outside the school gates? They wouldn't understand how hard it is to constantly feel on the back foot when it comes to your own child. The competitiveness is horrendous and Meg feels she's always spinning plates at that place: is her child performing well in class? Is her child well dressed and polite to his teachers? Is her child behaving properly and not beating the shit out of his classmates?

And it's not just about the kids, the adults are as bad. There's Mel who bounces up to the school gates wearing her size six fitness Lycra, her eyes slipping down occasionally when they're chatting, making little effort to hide the fact that she's noting the shape of Meg's hips. There's pretty Katya with the pixie haircut, which makes her look about eighteen, even though she's several years older than Meg. There's Amanda, who works full time, but whose perfectly behaved twin girls are always at school on time, wearing the right uniform with their faces scrubbed and their hair braided into neat plaits.

The congregation comes to the end of the hymn and the organ lingers on one last, quavering note.

'If only we hadn't been so late, we wouldn't be stuck right at the back,' hisses Nancy.

'Stop moaning,' whispers Ali. 'There's nothing we can do about it.'

'I can't see anything! We should have been here an hour ago.'

'At least we made it.'

'I hate churches – so fucking gloomy.' Nancy is shaking her head.

'Shut up.' Ali smacks Nancy on the forearm.

They sit back down onto the hard wooden pews. Meg hasn't been able to sing properly because there's a lump in her throat, a knot of panic in her stomach as she thinks about what her son might be getting up to. A sob bubbles up in her mouth, catching her by surprise and giving her no time to stifle it.

Ali nudges her. 'I know! I'm welling up too. Doesn't she look beautiful!'

Meg nods and sniffs, happy to pretend she's overcome with the emotion of the moment.

At the front of the church, the vicar is urging them to praise the Lord and celebrate the wonder of marriage, and Nancy tuts audibly. 'I hate religion,' she mutters.

'Don't we know it!' says Ali.

'I mean, Polly herself doesn't even believe in God!' Nancy's voice is loud enough for the couple in front to turn around and glare at them.

'Shh!' Meg says.

'I'm not sure why they're going through this rigmarole, when they could have a civil ceremony in a stately home,' Nancy continues, although more quietly.

'It's all about choice,' Ali whispers. 'Just because it isn't your thing, doesn't mean it's not right for other people.'

'It's not Polly's thing either! So hypocritical.'

'I bet you'll end up getting married in a church,' Meg whispers. 'You'll change your mind when the time comes and want a beautiful ceremony, just like this.' She can't actually imagine it though. Kind people might describe Nancy as down to earth, possibly practical and realistic. Others might be less complimentary: cynical, comes to Meg's mind, along with sarcastic and disparaging.

It suddenly occurs to her that Nancy is here alone. 'Where's Jeff?' she whispers. 'Wasn't he invited?'

Nancy shrugs. 'He was on the invitation.' But she doesn't look at Meg and she doesn't explain why her boyfriend of the last two years isn't sitting here beside them. Meg has met Jeff a couple of times, but doesn't know him well. She remembers chatting to him in a pub when he first started going out with Nancy – Meg was pregnant and the only sober person in the place, and she was very aware that he was talking down to her, assuming she wouldn't understand the finer points of what he was saying. He was right, because now she can't remember what he was telling her, only that he was being massively condescending.

Despite all that, Meg feels sorry for him: going out with Nancy must be bloody hard work. Even though he was invited, he probably made a deliberate decision not to come this weekend, needing some downtime away from his bolshy girlfriend.

'I will *never* get married in a church.' Nancy says now, crossing her arms in front of her chest. 'I'd rather stick needles in my eyes.'

Meg sighs. Nancy is a firebrand of a friend.

CHAPTER FOUR

M eg feels a hand on her arm and turns to find a girl grinning at her; the face may be vaguely familiar, yet she can't place her.

'Wasn't that a beautiful service!'

'Absolutely!' Meg smiles back, desperately wondering who this girl is.

The guests have spilled out of the church and are gathering in groups on the grass and pathway, while an energetic little photographer leaps around Polly and Adam, snapping away as he directs them into a variety of different poses. 'Now, let's have you looking at each other,' he calls. 'That's it! Lots of smiles! And back to me, this time – arm around her shoulder please, Adam. Turn a little to the left!'

The newly-weds have been speaking to their guests as they emerge from the church, turning to hug some people, exclaiming in delight at the sight of others, waving at those who aren't close by. But the photographer wants their undivided attention, and makes frantic shooing motions with one hand, as an elderly man tries to approach Polly.

'I'll be free in a minute!' she calls. 'We're only having a few photos here – it won't take long. Most of them will be done at the reception.'

Meg is caught up in a crowd, unable to move forwards or backwards.

'It's like a school reunion!' someone is saying. 'Hey, Jim! God, it's been years!'

'Lucie!' someone else is yelling. 'How have you been?'

Meg still can't remember the name of the girl who is now clinging onto her arm. Janey? Jade? She thinks they might have done English together, in the first year – or maybe she was someone's flatmate. They obviously weren't particularly close, but it's embarrassing she can't remember a thing about her. She opts for general chit-chat that won't give her away. 'Isn't this wonderful!' she says. 'You look fantastic.'

'Ah, thanks! You too,' the girl says. 'I do love a traditional church wedding.'

Ahead of them on the path, Nancy has wrapped herself around handsome Toby – Meg has no trouble remembering who he is – and there, standing behind him, are Luke and Daniel. Meg catches her breath and turns around to face the girl beside her. She can feel her cheeks colouring and, when she speaks, her voice sounds squeaky. 'Yes, me too! Church weddings are so romantic. Have you had one?' *What is she going on about? A church wedding isn't just one of those things you have!* She ought to make a joke about what she's just said, but the words won't come.

Luckily, the girl rescues her.

'Oh no, I'm still young, free and single. Or most of the time anyway. I'm sort of seeing someone, but it's quite casual. I really like him, but he works away a lot, and we have our separate groups of friends, so we don't...'

As she nods and pretends to listen, Meg steps to the left and turns her head slightly, so she can look past the girl's shoulder.

One of the twins has grown a hipster beard, but she doesn't have a clue which of them it is; at least she'll be able to tell the difference between them when she speaks to them later – *if* she speaks to them. Blood is racing around her body, thundering across her chest, making her temples throb. She's being ridiculous – of course she'll have to speak to them, otherwise it would look really weird. Anyway, it was years ago. So long ago, it almost feels like she was a different person.

The girl whose name escapes Meg – although Jade rings a bell – is looking at her, smiling, her head tipped to one side. She has clearly just asked a question.

'Sorry?'

'I said, what about you? Are you married?'

'Oh! Yes, I've been married a few years now. Two children.'

'Wow, amazing! Good for you.'

Telling those boys apart was virtually impossible back at Leeds. She remembers a handful of snapshot drunken moments from the night she first met them – everyone had been in that gloomy cellar bar, on the other side of the hospital.

The twins were teasing her. Several pints of lager to the wind, she'd been betting Luke she could tell him apart from Daniel. Or was it Daniel she could tell apart from Luke? She now has no idea, but knows she lost the bet and had a pint of cider thrust into her hand and was forced neck it. She has an awful feeling she threw most of it back up again shortly afterwards, when a big group of them were on the way home to the halls of residence. It's likely both of these handsome twins will have forgotten about the cellar incident, although Luke can't have forgotten about that other night, a few months later.

The girl – actually Janey seems more likely – puts a hand on Meg's forearm and starts to speak again. 'Just look at those two! Aren't they *the* most beautiful couple.'

Polly and Adam are standing on the church steps. He is

saying something to her and she's smiling, looking up at him with an expression full of so much love that it makes Meg's heart swell. They really are a gorgeous couple.

The photographer has finished dashing off shots with the church in the background and finally lowers his camera and steps back to allow the bride and groom to walk down the path, hand in hand. A wisp of blonde hair has fallen out of Polly's bun, but – as with everything about her – it looks artful and styled rather than messy. She is swiping at it carelessly with her hand and Meg can see the wedding band on the third finger of her left hand, glinting in the pale sunlight.

She turns again to Adam, laughing now at something he's saying, standing on her tiptoes to kiss him quickly on the lips. He is taller than Meg expected, but definitely better looking in real life than he was in all the social media posts she's seen. He has his arm around Polly's shoulder and his face is turned towards his new wife, his brown fringe drooping across his left eye.

'That dress is stunning!' says Janey or Jade. 'It's much more elegant than a traditional wedding dress, don't you think? Trust her to do something so classy.'

Polly is wearing a full-length sheath dress with miniature pearls sewn into the material. She has a bolero jacket over the top – essential in today's temperatures, even though the sun is trying its hardest to warm them – and the overall effect is effortlessly chic. Meg often wishes she'd worn something more sophisticated for her own wedding: her dress was quite old fashioned, with leg of mutton sleeves, intricate beading on the bodice and a short train which swept along the aisle behind her.

She had wanted to have her hair up like Polly's is now, maybe with flowers woven through it, but her mother had been horrified when Meg suggested something like that instead of a traditional veil. 'Every bride needs a veil!' she'd insisted. 'It adds a sense of mystery when you walk down the aisle.'

It had been the same with the dress: 'It has to be full length,' her mother had said. 'You can't have some silly little short thing. That would be far too frivolous. Anyway, you haven't got the legs for it.'

So, although she started out looking at many different options – and tried on dozens of outfits – Meg hadn't been particularly surprised when she ended up getting the sort of dress which she knew her mother had expected her to wear all along.

'They *are* paying for it,' she'd said to Joe. 'So, it's not really my decision to make.' It hadn't been an issue at the time and she'd loved every second of their wedding day.

But all these years later, she can't help feeling a twinge of disappointment as she looks at the stylish curve of Polly's dress, then thinks of the official wedding picture of herself and Joe, which sits on the windowsill in their sitting room. In that silver-framed photograph, they look very formal – standing stiffly to attention, side by side, with Meg clutching a small bouquet of pale pink roses, and the veil pushed back awkwardly from her forehead so that it sits slightly askew.

Although they're both smiling, they look as if they've been ordered to do so, on pain of death. That had almost certainly been the case: their wedding photographer – found, interviewed and employed by Meg's mother – was a bossy middle-aged woman who sloped off every few minutes to have a fag.

Meg had found her intimidating, but did what the woman told her to do and tried not to get irritated when she disappeared, leaving her and Joe standing around for what felt like ages. She told herself she just had to be patient, and it would be worth it: this was their big day, but the photographer was the expert and knew how to best capture it.

With hindsight, Meg realises that the woman didn't particularly care whether or not the happy couple looked as if they were having a good time on their special day; she was just there to shoot the agreed number of images and knock back some glasses of free fizz before heading off to her next job.

In contrast, Polly and Adam's photographer may be getting in everyone's way, but he's making sure he gets the sort of pictures which the happy couple will love looking back on, in years to come. While there will be many posed, relatively formal photographs to keep both sets of parents happy, there will also be dozens of others which will show them naturally relaxed and joyful, catching them unawares as they talk to their friends, looking as if they really are having the time of their lives.

'Oh, to be that much in love!' Janey or Jade is saying. 'They are *so* lucky. I always think that you can tell right from the beginning which marriages are going to last – there's just some special chemistry going on. Those two have definitely got it. They're going to be together *forever!*'

Meg looks around her, but Luke has disappeared now – if it is Luke. Nancy is talking to an older couple and Ali has moved away as well, she's now halfway down the path hugging a woman in a massive hat. Meg needs to circulate; there are definitely people here she should be talking to. She gently tries to pull her arm away, but Janey or Jade's fingers are clinging on tightly.

'So, where do you live?' she's asking. 'Did you have a long journey here this morning? I'm based in Bristol, which was handy – although the traffic on the M4 is always bad around Newport. But I made sure I left in plenty of time, and at least they didn't decide to hold the wedding in north Wales! That would have been a trek and a half.'

'I'm in London. But the journey was fine.' Meg waves

energetically at Ali and the woman in the hat, despite the fact that neither of them is looking at her. 'Lovely to bump into you again,' she says to Janey or Jade. 'I must just go and say hello to those two. See you at the reception!'

When she gets to Ali's side, she realises she knows the woman in the extravagant hat. She was one of Ali's friends from Leeds. 'Georgie, how are you?' she exclaims. 'It's so lovely to see you.'

The woman's brow wrinkles briefly, but clearly Meg's name isn't popping into her head. 'Hi!' she says. 'Goodness, you look... well.'

Meg chooses to ignore that. Over the last few years, being told she looks 'well' has too often been code for something else entirely, when people she hasn't seen for a while are unable to stop their eyes flicking downwards towards her post-baby belly. But sod it, she isn't going to be made to feel bad today. 'Thanks!' she smiles. 'You too! What a beautiful hat.'

Georgie's hand is still protectively on Ali's shoulder, and Meg briefly wonders if these two have history. Ali never made any secret of the fact that she was gay, but it wasn't something they ever discussed.

As far as Meg is aware, Ali wasn't in a relationship during their time at Leeds – she didn't even have any flings – although, in their final year, she forged a close friendship with one of her tutors, Maria Glenn. At the time, Meg presumed the two women had been drawn together because they shared a common interest: Ali was one of only a few female students in the engineering department at Leeds, while Maria was the only female lecturer there. But later, it occurred to Meg that the two women might have been lovers; she saw them out at dinner together once, their heads bent towards each other, Maria reaching across the table, her hand resting on Ali's forearm.

Then, a couple of weeks later, they went away for two days, to London for some careers conference.

Meg has never asked Ali about her lovers, because it's none of her business. When they were at uni, it might have been one of those things that would come up during a drunken evening, but it didn't and Meg didn't pry – the subject would have to have been raised by Ali, and it never was. Or at least, not with her. All these years later, Meg suspects that if anyone knows about Ali's love life, it will be Polly. Polly seems to know virtually everything there is to know about all of them.

Meg knows little about Ali's background, but did wonder if her parents disapproved of her because of her sexuality. They lived in Devon, but never came to visit Ali in Leeds and she stayed up there during the holidays. She didn't speak about her family and, if anyone asked questions about her life before university, her answers were brief and vague. There were rumours Ali had been at the centre of a big family row, after which she fell out with her father and was told never to darken the family door again, but Meg couldn't remember where she'd heard that.

'That Toby really is the one who got away.' Nancy is suddenly at her side. 'I always thought he was a gorgeous boy, but now he's a bloody Adonis.'

A short woman wearing a fuchsia pink dress, steps back into Meg, stamping on her toe, then turns and thrusts a box into her hand. 'Confetti!' she stage-whispers. 'Give it out!'

Meg opens the box and begins to tip pink flakes onto outstretched palms. 'Let me have some!' says Ali. 'Quickly!'

Polly and Adam are starting to walk away from the church towards the lychgate and, as confetti flutters around them, the little photographer leaps backwards down the path, snapping away.

'Congratulations!' people are calling. 'You look amazing!'

'We'll see you all later!' Polly says. 'Thank you so much for being here!'

Down on the road, a horse and carriage wait to transport the happy couple to the reception. It's only when Adam has helped his bride up onto the shiny leather seat and the horse has started to clop slowly away, the guests cheering and waving, that Meg realises she is still holding a tight fistful of confetti. She opens her hand and lets the pink flakes spill around her feet, hoping no one else will notice.

Guests drift out of the churchyard into the road, chatting, laughing and moving towards parked cars. The sun is still out and – even though it's a couple of weeks after the shortest day of the year and there are no leaves on the trees – the world is bright and colourful.

'I can't understand why they ordered a horse and carriage!' Nancy is beside Meg again, swiping through photos she has taken on her phone. 'The hotel is just around that corner, they could have walked it in three minutes.'

'It's romantic to be driven there like that,' Meg says.

Nancy rolls her eyes. 'And expensive.'

'Don't be such a cynic,' says Ali. 'Just because you don't have a shred of romance in you, doesn't mean other people's lives have to be equally miserable.'

Although the hotel is close, there are so many cars parked around the church and the lanes leading away from it, that it takes nearly twenty minutes for them to drive there. As they eventually find a space in the hotel car park, Ali unbuckles her seat belt and breathes out in relief. 'I'm gagging for a drink. Let's grab our cases and get checked in, then we can relax and enjoy the rest of the day.'

'We need to take the present in,' Nancy says. 'Where is it, Al?'

SARAH EDGHILL

Meg sees something flash across Ali's face; it could be confusion, but looks more like panic.

'The present?'

'Yes, the wedding present – for Adam and Polly!'

'I think... is it on the back seat?' Ali turns and looks over her shoulder.

'Not that I can see,' Meg says. 'Did you put it in the boot?'

Ali is looking like a trapped animal. 'No, it's not in there.'

'You don't mean...?' Nancy's mouth drops open. 'Please tell me you *have* got the present, Ali. That it's somewhere in this car?'

'Actually, no.' Ali puts her hands up to her face. 'Shit, I'm really sorry. I have an awful feeling I forgot to pick it up. It was on the kitchen table this morning, but I rushed out, because I was a bit late leaving...'

'Jesus!' says Nancy. 'I don't believe this. How could you forget it?'

'I was in a hurry!'

'I'm sure it doesn't matter...' Meg begins.

'This is crazy!' Nancy says. 'Honestly, Ali. How could you leave it behind? Are you being straight with us, or did you forget to go out and buy it?'

'Yes, of course I bought it!' Ali's eyes are blazing. 'How dare you! I went on a special trip to buy the bloody thing, last weekend. And I wrapped it in fancy wedding paper and I wrote out a card from all of us.'

The joint present had seemed like a good idea when Meg suggested it. With three of them contributing, they could get something substantial for Polly. There had been long-winded email exchanges as they studied the list from the official wedding registry and tossed around suggestions.

Meg was keen to get her something for the flat. 'How about a fancy food processor? She loves to cook!'

42

Nancy had been dismissive. 'God, that's too domestic and boring. I think we ought to get her something wild and extravagant. I saw an amazing antique glass chandelier in Camden Market the other week.'

'Hard to find a decent place for something like that in a two-bed flat in Battersea,' pointed out Ali.

'And you say I'm the one who's lacking a sense of romance!'

'It's not very practical, though, is it Nancy?' Meg had felt obliged to add.

'How about a spa weekend?' offered Ali.

'I do think it might be better to get them something they can keep and use?' Meg had been really keen on the idea of a food processor. She and Joe had added one onto their wedding list, and she'd been disappointed when no one bought it. She'd half hoped her parents would get it for them, but for some weird reason they avoided the official list altogether and gave Meg and Joe a set of crystal champagne boules which had never been taken out of the box. There wasn't much call for expensive glassware when you were running around after small children in East Finchley. A food processor to blitz all the baby food to a mush, on the other hand, would have come in rather useful.

'A weekend at a spa would be fun for both of them,' Ali had insisted. 'A chance to get away and be pampered. What's not to like?'

'Adam isn't a "spa" kind of bloke.' Nancy again.

'I'm not sure men really like all that pampering.' For once, Meg had agreed with Nancy. She only had Joe to hold up as an example, but he never so much as slapped moisturiser on his cheeks, so she couldn't imagine him sloping around a posh spa, wearing a white towelling robe and fluffy slippers.

Eventually, they'd decided to go for a coffee machine which was so sophisticated and offered such a long list of different caffeine-related options, that it was only one step down from having a barista living in your kitchen. 'At least we know she'll really use one of those,' Ali had said.

But now, the three of them are at the wedding, while the coffee machine is sitting in a carefully wrapped box, 150 miles away, on Ali's kitchen table in Greenwich.

'I knew buying something together was a mistake,' says Nancy. 'I should have got them a present on my own. Then at least I would have been able to hand it over *on the day*!'

'I don't think they'll mind,' Meg says, trying to catch Ali's eye and smile to show solidarity. 'They won't even look at all the presents until they get back from honeymoon. I know we didn't. My parents took them away from the reception and stacked them up in their garage and–'

'We agreed you'd be the one to get the present, Ali,' Nancy interrupts, 'because you insisted you had the time and would get it done.'

'I could easily have done it,' mutters Meg. She'd been slightly offended when the job was given to Ali. Meg loves shopping, and has always thought she has a real knack when it comes to choosing the right present for the right person.

'And I *did* get it sorted!' snaps Ali. 'Don't give me a hard time, Nancy, I'm really up against it at work and have had no time off recently, and if you're so organised, why didn't you offer to go out and sort the present?'

'Because I'm working bloody hard too! Yes, we all know you work long hours and do all that travelling, but my life isn't exactly a piece of piss. Although clearly teachers aren't *nearly* as important as people who work in industry.'

'I'm not saying that, don't be so sensitive.'

'I'm not being sensitive! I'm just pointing out you're not the only one on the planet who's busy and trying to hold it all together.'

'It really doesn't matter,' Meg cuts in, desperately. 'We can send it to them, by courier or something, so they get it when they come back from honeymoon.'

'But the whole point is they won't have it on the day!' Nancy sighs over-dramatically. 'We're turning up empty handed to their bloody wedding. It's disappointing, that's all. Really disappointing. I thought we could rely on you, Ali.'

'Jesus, I'm not one of your Year 9 psychos! Stop patronising me.'

'I'm sure Polly won't mind...' starts Meg.

'I'm not patronising you. If I was, believe me, you'd really know about it.'

'Yes, I bet I would.' Ali snaps.

They sit in silence, listening to the Audi engine tick as it cools down, watching a couple who have just parked beside them, get out of their car and wheel a suitcase towards the hotel entrance. Meg can see the tension in Ali's jaw, the slight flutter of a muscle under her left eye. Nancy has crossed her arms in front of her chest and is staring out of the passenger window, resentment and irritation rolling off her in waves.

'Right, let's not worry about the present now,' says Meg, when she can bear the angry silence no longer. She leans forward and puts one hand on each of their shoulders. 'What's done is done, let's get our things and go in, shall we? This place looks amazing! What a great venue for a wedding reception. Staying here tonight is going to be a real treat.'

Neither of the others says a word.

CHAPTER FIVE

The waiter holding a tray of champagne flutes seems barely into his teens. His hair is slicked back from his face with an excess of gel, his cheeks are littered with pimples and the red waistcoat with the hotel insignia on the front is so big it's falling off his shoulders: he looks like his mum has packed him off for his first day at secondary school in an older brother's cast-offs.

Meg smiles at him encouragingly when he holds out the tray, the glasses tinkling as his hands shake. 'Thank you!' she says. 'You're doing a great job.' She is trying to offer moral support: show the boy that she understands how awkward it must be for him, having to stand here in his formal uniform, serving all these loud people dressed in their middle-class finery. But he clearly thinks she's being sarcastic; his cheeks turn pink and he glares at her.

Ali reaches for a glass and clinks it against Meg's. 'Cheers,' she says. 'God, I really need this.'

'Have you got a soft drink?' Nancy asks the boy.

The other two stare at her. 'What the hell?' Ali says. 'Are you serious?'

'We're going to be drinking for the next ten hours –

probably more – so I don't intend to be paralytic by mid-afternoon. Anyway, I hate drinking at lunchtime; it means I fall asleep. I'm going to start slowly.'

'That's very sensible,' says Meg, finishing her champagne and reaching out for another full glass before the pubescent waiter has time to turn away. She herself has no intention of being sensible. In fact, her aim for this afternoon is to drink as much expensive champagne as she can, partly because someone else is paying for it, but also because she can't actually remember the last time she got properly pissed.

Normally she doesn't have more than one glass of wine in an evening, maybe two if it's a Saturday night, otherwise it makes the early starts with Tallulah so much worse. It's hard enough dragging herself out of bed every day before the bloody birds have even woken up, but it's so much worse trying to do it with a head that feels like it has been pumped full of molten lead. A few weekends ago, she and Joe opened a second bottle of wine while watching something on Netflix – at the time it seemed like a very good idea – but the next morning she felt so rough that she lost her rag and yelled when Tallulah dropped her bowl of cereal and milk onto the sofa. They both ended up in tears and Meg felt like the worst mother in the world for hours.

Another waiter – this one possibly old enough to be doing GCSEs – is handing Nancy a glass of something which is also sparkling but slightly darker than the gloriously pale-yellow champagne. 'Thanks,' she says. 'Anyway, Ali, I seem to remember you saying in the past that if people need alcohol to have a good time, it's a sign of weakness and social insecurity.'

'Fuck off,' says Ali, draining her own glass.

Meg watches as Nancy takes a sip of whatever she has been given; probably elderflower – every non-alcoholic alternative nowadays seems to revolve around elderflower in some form. It certainly isn't like the old Nancy to be sensible on an occasion like this.

Meg thinks back to their countless drunken nights out at Leeds, too many for them to now be anything more than a jumbled collision of partial memories. Meg had rarely touched alcohol before she arrived at university: her parents weren't big drinkers and, although she'd had the occasional can of lager at parties, it never did much for her.

During her first few days at Leeds, she soon realised she would need to up her game if she was going to fit in with these loud new friends she was making and she certainly didn't want to be the only sober fresher in the bar. But although she began to drink more often and in greater quantities, she'd remained an unadventurous drinker and nearly always stuck to wine.

Nancy, on the other hand, was hardcore: she would invariably get tanked up on vodka while they were getting ready, then move onto wine when they went out, or beer if that was cheaper, before finishing the night with shots. If she ever ended up with shocking hangovers, Meg didn't witness them, maybe because they never shared a flat. But although she had no idea how it was possible for someone to binge-drink so much and not suffer for it afterwards, Nancy wasn't the sort of friend she could chat to about something like that. She would have given Meg one of her withering looks and left her feeling like the naïve innocent she knew she was.

When they were introduced, all those years ago, Meg had found Nancy cold and distant and she was surprised Polly had hooked up with her. Meg and Ali had been in the union bar, having a cheap night rather than going into town, and Polly texted to find out where they were. Ten minutes later, she appeared in the doorway, her arm looped through that of a tall girl with long auburn hair.

When Polly waved and came over to their table, dragging

the girl with her, Meg was struck by the negativity radiating from this stranger; she was smiling, but there was no warmth in it. Her eyes flickered from Ali to Meg and back again, but it was as if she was scanning items on a supermarket shelf.

Ever since she'd arrived at uni, Meg had grown used to meeting new people who also seemed keen to meet her. That was the thing about student life: you threw yourself into anything and everything and made an effort to smile and laugh and chat and flirt and do all the things you thought – at least hoped – made you an interesting person. Or Meg did. Even at the time, she realised that said quite a lot about her own insecurity and neediness – but she also knew she was by no means alone.

But this girl with the striking auburn hair was different. She was the same age as they were, halfway through her second year, but seemed older. Meg couldn't now remember where Polly had met her, but – being Polly – she pulled Nancy into their little group and integrated her effortlessly and enthusiastically.

Nancy did mellow as the others got to know her better, but Meg never stopped feeling inadequate in her company. She also felt a little bit judged, and being with Nancy made her more conscious of how she was behaving, more humiliated by the occasional stupid comment which came out of her own mouth before she could stop herself. To cover up her embarrassment, she played the fool – laughing at herself and the idiotic things she did, before hard-nosed Nancy had a chance to do so.

This was a persona she'd already been working on since she started at Leeds: she knew she was never going to be the beautiful one – that was Polly; or the clever one – that was Ali; so she would be the funny one. It wasn't hard: she *was* funny, people had always laughed at her jokes and her little asides, and from there it was only a small step towards self-deprecation. Meg didn't mind; it was easier to be the one to bring up her own failings, than to pretend not to care if she was the butt of other people's jokes.

But although being with Nancy got easier as they all got to know each other, Meg never felt totally relaxed in her company, and the relationship between the two of them felt very different to the one she had with Ali and Polly. There was something slightly intimidating about Nancy's self-assurance; it made Meg feel like she was the runner-up in a game she didn't even know she was playing.

A few weeks after meeting Nancy, she mentioned this to Ali, hoping to learn she wasn't the only one who was struggling with this self-confident, sardonic girl who was suddenly part of their friendship group. But Ali had been surprised and didn't seem to get it; she just shrugged and told Meg she was being over-sensitive. Meg nodded and said she was sure Ali was right, pretending – as usual – to laugh it off.

The problem was, they were polar opposites. Meg hated being the centre of attention, Nancy loved it. Meg was deferential to authority and determined to work hard at university, Nancy didn't take any of it seriously and was forever copying up other people's notes because she'd missed lectures and tutorials.

Nancy was also a natural flirt and had a succession of boyfriends. Meg knew she herself was a bit of a prude – she'd only lost her virginity at the end of her first year at Leeds to her then boyfriend, Ed – but she was regularly shocked not just by Nancy's casual attitude towards sex, but by the way she discussed it in such detail afterwards. Hearing about Nancy's latest sexual exploits made Meg squirm with embarrassment and she had to work really hard not to show it.

The pimply young waiter is back, his tray full again, a dozen more champagne flutes jingling against each other.

'Where are the happy couple?' Ali is asking.

'Over there,' Nancy says. 'They must be frozen, they've been standing outside for ages having hundreds more photos taken, which they'll stick into an album and never look at again.'

'Cynic,' says Ali.

Polly and Adam are now surrounded by a circle of older relatives: undoubtedly a selection of aunts, uncles and second cousins twice removed, whom they don't know particularly well and haven't seen in years, but have felt obliged to invite.

Meg knows that every wedding has its quota of these: the distant family contingent who buy half a dozen tumblers from the John Lewis wedding list and turn up on the day, looking – and undoubtedly feeling – awkward. Her own parents had insisted on inviting a dozen of their friends to her wedding, as well as a battalion of elderly relatives, and Meg had felt irritated – and ever so slightly condemned – by certain members of the older generation, who hung around on the edges at the reception, looking as if they'd rather be elsewhere and tutting as her friends got progressively more drunk and rowdy.

Meg puts her empty glass on the waiter's trembling tray and takes another full one; they must be very small glasses because she's finishing them surprisingly fast. She sees Nancy raising one eyebrow at her and smiles. 'Cheers!' Meg tilts the glass in her direction before taking a sip.

Bugger Nancy. She can afford to be sensible: she goes out several nights a week, and can drink to excess without worrying that she'll feel like shit if she's woken up by a crying child in the night. Meg needs this, she reassures herself as the champagne slides deliciously down her throat: she deserves it.

CHAPTER SIX

The self-flushing toilet gives Meg such a shock when it gushes into action, that she leaps backwards and bangs her elbow on the cubicle door. Like everything else in this hotel, the ladies cloakroom is the ultimate in high-end sophistication. The sanitaryware is the highest quality porcelain, and above the shiny black floor tiles, the room has been decorated in rich reds and silvery greys, with subtle downlighting and flock wallpaper.

As she stands at the oval countertop basin, body-temperature water slides from the wall-mounted taps so silently that, at first, she doesn't even realise her hands are getting wet. There are stacks of fluffy white towels and, once she has dried her hands on one, Meg puts it back onto the pile before realising it needs to be tossed carelessly into one of the tall wicker laundry bins beneath the basins.

Against the far wall is a mirrored seating area with hairdryers, boxes of tissues and several bottles of Molton Brown hand cream. Meg sits down and rubs the thick lotion into her arms and across her chest, breathing in the rich, expensive scent, feeling pampered and special. Oh, to live this sort of lifestyle. Molton Brown isn't a brand she could ever justify using at home, although she has bought an Aldi rip-off version, which wasn't bad at all.

She briefly considers nicking one of these expensive bottles and taking it home, so she can decant the Aldi stuff into it and put in the downstairs loo, pretending to visitors that she's a Molton Brown sort of woman. Except there's nowhere to hide a bottle because her handbag is a blue clutch, just big enough for her phone, and she can't just brazenly walk out of here holding one. As she picks up the nearest bottle and imagines herself doing exactly that, the door behind her swings open and two women burst through it, talking over each other, the sound of laughter and clinking glasses following them through from the hotel reception.

Meg rubs more cream into her hands, listening as the women continue their conversation from adjacent cubicles.

'She's bloody stupid,' one is saying. 'He's been messing her about for years, but of course she refuses to see it. Believes she needs to stick with him for the sake of the kids.'

'What an arse,' says the other woman. 'I never liked him. But to be fair, she has let herself go a bit. She must have put on at least two stone since we saw them last year in Dubai.'

Meg leans forward and slips her cardigan off her shoulders before adjusting the straps of her dress, then pulls at the material as it wrinkles around her stomach. Have Ali and Nancy had a similar toilet cubicle conversation about her recently? She's seen them giving her the side eye, trying not to make it obvious they're judging her for the excess baby weight she can't shift.

Joe reassures her, telling her all the time that she's beautiful: 'You've given birth to two babies!' he reminded her the other week, after she'd made the mistake of stepping on the bathroom scales and was sitting on the edge of the bed in tears. 'Your body carried our children! I love it, and so should you.' He's a sweetheart, but it doesn't make her feel better.

She's wearing a new pair of shaper pants she ordered from M&S; although they're doing what it says on the tin – smoothing out her bulges – they're bloody uncomfortable. The waistband of the pants is starting to roll down and the leg holes are cutting into her thighs. She squirms in the seat and sighs, pulling the elasticated fabric away from her belly for a few seconds to give herself a chance to breathe.

It took weeks to find this dress for Polly's wedding. She went to so many shops and tried on dozens of dresses, all of which looked gorgeous on hangers, but, as soon as she wriggled them up over her hips in the changing rooms, every single one was disappointing. She stared at herself in numerous different store mirrors, seeing nothing except the bulges. She remembers reading an article somewhere about the mirrors in these places: how they're designed to deliberately flatter customers by slightly changing their shape, a bit like those fairground mirrors that make you look excessively tall and thin. But if that really is true, Meg has been shopping in the wrong stores – she looked short and fat in everything she tried on.

She eventually came across this dress in a local charity shop, just after Christmas, and thought it must be karma. The soft flimsy material wasn't ideal for an early January wedding, but it didn't drag or squeeze too much and she already had a cream cardigan that would go over the top. Plus, it was a pretty colour, and the neckline was low enough to be flattering but not obscene. As she handed over £7.50 to the assistant in Sue Ryder Care, she wasn't able to stop grinning: she'd been *meant* to find this dress and wear it to Polly's wedding, it was absolutely perfect. She tried it on for Joe, that evening, whirling around the bedroom, loving how the material floated out from the waist in an arc. Best of all, there was a faint blue and purple floral pattern on the cream background, which meant she could pair it with her trusty stilettos. It seemed as if fate made her step into that charity shop and, for the first time in a long while, she felt pretty and almost confident.

The two women have finally come out of the cubicles and are washing their hands in silently-flowing water then drying them on luxurious white towels. They throw them towards the wicker basket; one misses, but neither woman makes a move to pick it up from the floor.

'Did you see that the Masons have put their place on the market?' one of them says.

'God, yes. Ridiculously overpriced. But rumour has it, his business is going under.'

'Really? That's interesting. Explains why they're selling up. They've only been there a couple of years.'

Having fluffed their hair and examined their make-up in the mirrors, the women head towards the door. Neither of them acknowledges Meg or even glances in her direction. When they've gone, she sits back and sighs as she looks at herself in the mirror again, wondering if anyone else at this fancy wedding is wearing a second-hand dress they bought in a charity shop. It's so unlikely, it's laughable.

She still loves the dress and, deep down, knows she looks okay in it. But now she's here alongside all these beautiful svelte people, she can't stop judging herself again – and finding herself lacking in so many ways. If only Joe was here to bolster her confidence. 'You'd still be the most beautiful woman in the world, if you walked out of the front door wearing a bin liner,' he'd said a while ago, after she came back from another unsuccessful shopping trip.

'But I can't wear a bin liner to a wedding!'

'There's a first time for everything.' He'd winked at her, and she laughed, immediately feeling better.

But right now, Joe is many miles away, dealing with small children and domestic chaos, and Meg is in a posh hotel in Wales with some of her dearest friends, who have no idea how hard it is for her just to be here with them.

She has known these women for years and loves them, but it felt so strange in the car this morning, having to listen to Ali and Nancy talk about parties they'd been to and recent city break weekends where they drank too much local rosé. Meg's world now revolves around children and dealing with everyone else's needs apart from her own.

Since Ollie was born, five years ago, and Tallulah came along, three years later, her support network has consisted of other mothers: women she has met at antenatal groups and playgroups; women whose lives are similarly consumed by nappies and dribble and tantrums. Women who are mostly also still carrying baby weight and favour big floaty tops that cover up a multitude of sins. Women whose husbands are bit-part players in the new lives they are creating for themselves, which revolve around nurseries and soft play centres. Women who constantly put their backs out carrying overloaded changing bags and gathering up screaming toddlers before balancing them on one hip. Women whose lives are packed full of love, but also so very different to the lives of their university friends who think nothing of travelling for hours to attend sophisticated social engagements in swanky hotels.

'Fuck it,' Meg says out loud, to her reflection in the mirror. 'Fuck the lot of them.' She takes a deep breath and gets to her feet, wincing as the stiletto cuts into her heel again. She is here. She is away from home for just one night. She needs to make the most of it.

As she comes out of the ladies cloakroom, a waiter is walking past with a tray of full champagne flutes.

'Excuse me!' Meg smiles at him. 'Can I have one of those?'

She tips the glass up and empties it in three swallows, feeling a rush of adrenalin as the bubbles slide down her throat. Just what she needs: a bit of Dutch courage. She can't see anyone she knows out here in the hotel reception area, but she is going to go in search of a familiar face. She will smile and sparkle and throw herself into conversations; she will push her shoulders back and hold her chin up high and let those constricting shaper pants do their work. She will enjoy this bloody wedding if it kills her.

CHAPTER SEVEN

As always, Polly manages to make Meg feel special.

'Look at you!' she cries, throwing her arms around her. 'You look wonderful, Meg. I've missed you so much, it's been far too long. How are those gorgeous children of yours?'

Meg hugs her back, luxuriating in the familiar shape of her friend's arms and shoulders, glad to be the focus of Polly's world – even if it is only for a few seconds. 'They're fine, we're all good. Joe sends his love,' she says, trying not to crush her cheek against Polly's hair, with its intricately woven strands of pearls.

'I'm sorry he couldn't be here as well, but it's lovely to have you with us,' Polly is saying. 'Adam, come and say hello to Meg! I can't believe you two still haven't met after all this time.'

Meg holds out her hand, but Adam is already moving in to kiss her on the cheek, his fingers resting gently on her forearm. 'I've heard so much about you,' he says, smiling with such sincerity that Meg feels herself flushing. She has seen plenty of photos of this man on Polly's social media accounts over the last couple of years but, in the flesh, he really is ridiculously handsome. In less than a second, she takes in his prominent cheekbones, strong forehead and perfectly straight nose, and stares up into deep blue eyes that make her feel as if she's the centre of his universe.

'Me too!' she says, clearing an irritating croak in her throat. 'I mean, I've heard so much about you as well. From Polly.' She inwardly cringes at her own idiocy; of course she has heard about him from Polly – he's her fiancé. Who else would be filling her in on the life and times of Adam Harris?

But if he finds her awkwardness amusing, he doesn't show it. He is every bit as effortlessly relaxed and charming as his new wife, who is standing beside him, moving along the waiting line of their friends: kissing, hugging, making each one of them feel as if they're contributing something hugely valuable to this big day. 'Ali! You look fabulous. Great dress, that colour really suits you. Thanks for driving everyone down – how was the journey?'

'It was fine. We would have driven a million miles to be here with you today, Pol.'

'Aw, that's so lovely! But how crazy is it, that it takes a wedding to get us all in the same room!' Polly laughs.

'I know. We're useless,' says Ali. 'Congratulations Mrs Harris.'

'That still sounds so strange.' Polly turns to Adam and squeezes his arm. 'Mrs Harris! I feel I need to do some more growing up before I can start answering to that.'

A man standing beside them leans closer. 'Remember, Polly, you will only ever be the *lesser* Mrs Harris!' The bride and groom both burst out laughing and, as the man turns away, he catches Meg's eye and winks. 'Wait until you meet the mother-in-law!' he stage-whispers.

'You look stunning,' Ali tells Polly.

'You really do.' Meg moves forward to throw her arms around her friend again. 'I'm so happy for you.'

Adam moves along to hug Ali, and they stand with their arms loosely around each other, laughing about something.

They clearly know each other well. Meg feels a stab of jealousy, remembering how Nancy mentioned looking after this man's dog for a weekend. They all seem very close; when did Nancy get to know Adam well enough to dog-sit for him? What is this story he's telling Ali, right now? She's listening to him, rapt, her mouth slightly open, leaning forward in his arms as he reaches a punchline that makes her throw back her head and scream with laughter. He is laughing as well, clearly enjoying the effect his words have had.

'That's crazy!' Ali is laughing. 'I can't believe he never found out?'

To cover her embarrassment at feeling left out of all the conversations going on around her, Meg lifts her glass to her lips, but she has tilted it almost upside down before she realises it's empty. She lowers it again quickly, hoping no one has noticed. She looks around for the pimply waiter, but there isn't a hotel waistcoat in sight.

Polly has now moved along to where Nancy has been waiting and the two of them are hugging tightly, Nancy whispering something in her ear.

Adam breaks away from Ali and stands beside them, his head slightly on one side. Meg has another chance to look at him, unobserved; he reminds her of someone, but she can't think who. It's someone she has seen recently – most probably just an actor in some TV drama. She struggles to come up with a name, but having downed three glasses of champagne in a very short space of time, things are already a bit foggy. She holds the chilled glass against her cheek, hoping it will help calm the heat flaring across her face: champagne always does this to her, but it's so long since she drank any of it, she'd forgotten. She realises she's swaying slightly as she studies Adam's profile. He looks a bit like the guy in that Harlan Coben detective series she and Joe recently watched on Netflix, but that's not who she was thinking of. Maybe a footballer? Or someone on *Love Island*?

'We've bought you a wedding present,' Nancy is saying to Polly. 'But unfortunately, it got left behind on Ali's kitchen table. Which means you'll only be able to open it when you get back from honeymoon.'

Meg sees irritation briefly flash across Ali's face, before she laughs. 'Yes, it's all my fault, I'm really sorry. But it will be worth the wait! I'll make sure to get it to you as soon as you're back.'

Nancy steps away from Polly and glares at Ali. Yet again, Meg is desperate to change the subject and keep the peace.

'Do you know where you're going on honeymoon?' she asks quickly. Surely these two won't carry on going at each other, now they're in the hotel, with the bride and groom standing right here in front of them?

'No idea,' says Polly. 'But apparently, I need to pack for warm sunny days. Even at this time of year, the temperature won't drop dramatically at night. It will be so good to get some sunshine after the rubbish weather we had over Christmas.'

Adam puts his arm around her waist and pulls her towards him. 'Whatever the temperature, I'll be working hard to keep you warm,' he grins, moving in and kissing her ear.

Polly shakes her head and raises her eyes at Meg, but she's laughing as well. 'Thanks again for being here, girls,' she says. 'I love you all!'

'Love you too!' they chorus, as she turns away to greet someone else. In the gap she leaves behind, Nancy turns towards Adam and Meg is surprised by the expression on her face; the natural, wide smile she had for Polly disappears, and all of a sudden there's a flash of something else there.

'Adam, how are you?' she asks.

'Fine. Yes, all good.' He leans forward and they touch cheeks. Meg can't see his face but, in an instant, they pull away from each other again and Adam has moved further along, following Polly onto the next group of friends. Nancy turns and her eyes meet Meg's.

'What?' she asks.

'Nothing!' Meg is immediately flustered – she hadn't realised she was staring. Bloody champagne. 'So, you looked after his dog?' she asks. She isn't sure why she has suddenly brought this up again, but can't think of anything else to say.

'Yes, Meg. I looked after his dog.' The look Nancy gives her is on the freezing side of cool. She raises one eyebrow. 'What about it?'

'Oh, nothing! I was just thinking how nice that would be. To look after a dog. I think the kids would really like that.' Meg goes to take another sip from her glass, before remembering – yet again – that the bloody thing is empty. She stands awkwardly, twirling the stem of her glass between her thumb and forefinger.

Maybe she will offer to help out with Adam's cute little spaniel at some stage: how much trouble could it be to have an animal in the house for a weekend? She has never been keen on the idea of owning pets – life at home is too chaotic already – but Ollie and Tallulah would love it if they had a dog to stay for a couple of days; it would be good for them to have an animal for company and to learn how to look after it.

An image briefly flashes through her mind of Ollie in the park a couple of weeks ago: a little Jack Russell was sniffing around by the benches and Ollie had gone over to it, trying to grab it and stroke the wiry fur on its neck. Meg wasn't paying attention and her head was turned away as she chatted to one of the other parents. Suddenly there was a high-pitched yelp and, when she whipped her head back around, she saw the little dog limping towards the far side of the playground, moving as quickly as it could on three legs, with the fourth held awkwardly off the ground.

'What happened?' she asked Ollie. He just shrugged and walked away. There was a stick in his hand and he tossed it into the bushes. A young woman was pushing her daughter on a nearby swing and Meg saw she was shaking her head and glaring at her. Meg glared back before turning and resuming her conversation; she had no idea what that was all about – some of the parents who brought their children to the playground could be massively over-protective.

It was only later, when they were walking home, that she thought again about the little dog. 'Did you see what happened to it?' she asked Ollie. 'Did it run into something?' Her son just shrugged and didn't answer. He was walking slightly ahead of her and didn't bother turning around. 'Maybe it had hurt its leg earlier,' she said, almost to herself. 'Or it got something stuck in its paw.' She didn't mention the incident to Joe that evening, there didn't seem much point. But she couldn't help thinking about the stick she'd watched Ollie throw into the bushes.

Ali has now turned back towards them. 'That was unnecessary, Nancy,' she says.

'What?'

'You know what. You had to get in that little dig about the bloody present, didn't you.'

'Let's not do this here!' Meg whispers. 'Nancy, we were just grateful Ali sorted out the present for us, and Polly obviously doesn't mind. Let's forget about it and get another drink. Come on, Ali, your glass is empty. Where's that boy with the champagne?'

'For God's sake, stop trying to make everything better, Meg,' Nancy snaps. 'Why do you always have to be the bloody peacekeeper?'

A different waiter walks past, his tray loaded with full bottles of champagne. Ali reaches out and grabs one of the bottles, smiling sweetly at the boy as he walks away again. 'Here we go,' she says. 'Hold your glass steady, Meg. Nancy, have you had any of this yet?'

Nancy doesn't answer, she just shakes her head at the pair of them.

'I think you need a drink,' Ali says. 'It might help you lighten up a bit. This is a wedding, Nancy, not a funeral.'

'Fuck off,' says Nancy. 'You're being bloody irritating today.'

'Right back at you,' Ali says, raising her glass. 'Cheers!'

Although Meg has allowed her glass to be topped up again, she ought to slow down. She can't remember the last time she drank this much. Even at Christmas, she doesn't let herself overdo it, knowing she'll need to keep her wits about her because the kids get hyper and, despite going to bed later than usual, they'll have her up before dawn. The Christmas just past was no exception. Tallulah was too young to really understand what the festivities are all about, but she still picked up on the excitement and the fact that she was going to get presents. She was bouncing up and down on Meg and Joe's bed at 4.30am on Christmas Day, yelling 'Fa Kissmus!' into their ears.

But sod it, this is different: Meg won't have to get up early tomorrow. There will be no needy screams dragging her from sleep in the middle of the night, no early morning wails for attention, no wet beds or heavy, sodden nappies to be dealt with. Meg will be able to sleep as late as she wants. So actually, why not make the most of it?

She takes another long, satisfying sip of champagne, tipping her head back as she does so and squinting up at the sparkling chandelier above their heads in the crowded hotel reception area. But the movement is a little too sudden, because dizziness twists the scene above her head, making the ceiling swoop nastily to one side. She quickly looks down again and giggles.

Nancy glares at her, but Meg decides not to care. She has no idea what's wrong with Nancy, or why she's in a foul mood.

Maybe she actually wanted Jeff to come with her today, but he refused – or just had something else on.

She was fine until they had that argument about the wedding present in the car, but it can't just have been that? The thing with Adam was weird too; maybe she just doesn't like him very much? It would be typical of Nancy to take against someone for no reason. Meg feels sorry for him: if Adam has the slightest bit of sensitivity in him – which he clearly does – he'll be well aware that he's not Nancy's favourite person, because her signature negative vibes will be smacking him in the face. Has Polly picked up on any of this? Hopefully not. The last thing any bride needs to think about on her wedding day, is that one of her closest friends has taken against her husband.

The happy couple are now surrounded by another group, a few feet away, and there is much back-slapping and hugging going on. Meg leans sideways and whispers in Ali's ear. 'Adam is very handsome.'

Ali nods. 'Guess so.'

'Not your type?' whispers Meg. She isn't sure why she's doing this. But she's definitely emboldened by alcohol; slightly demob-happy at being away and feeling like a grown-up who's on a weekend pass. For some reason, at this precise moment, she wants to get a reaction from Ali.

Her friend turns and frowns at her. 'What do you mean?'

'You know!' Meg nudges her and points at Adam with her glass. 'Him, he's really gorgeous.'

Ali raises her eyebrows. 'Yes, Meg. No one could argue that Adam is anything other than gorgeous.'

'But I suppose,' Meg ploughs on, keeping her voice so low that only Ali can hear her. '*Only* if you like that sort of thing.' She starts to laugh, but it turns into a silly little snigger, and she feels stupid.

'And your point is?' Ali asks.

'No point. No point at all. Not one single point.'

Ali tuts and moves away, striking up a conversation with some people behind them. Nancy seems to have disappeared as well and Meg is left standing by herself.

Adam has said something and everyone is laughing, looking at each other, raising eyebrows, enjoying the spectacle. She is near enough to be able to hear the conversation, but Meg has missed what he said because she was whispering to Ali.

She shakes her head and takes a deep breath in, forcing herself to concentrate, then steps forward and lurks on the edge of the group. She doesn't know any of these people and she's never been good at inserting herself into a crowd of strangers, but it's amazing how quickly alcohol does away with most of life's usual inhibitions.

CHAPTER EIGHT

They don't sit down to eat until 3.30pm, by which time Meg has put away at least five glasses of champagne – or maybe six, she isn't sure – and only been offered two canapés, which are so miniscule that one of them slips out of her fingers and falls into her cleavage. 'Oops!' she giggles, scooping it out again and shovelling it into her mouth, before wiping a streak of cream cheese off the exposed skin at the top of her left breast and licking her finger. 'Silly me.'

'Meg, you need to slow down,' says Nancy, who still appears to be nursing the same untouched glass of elderflower. 'How much have you had?'

'Not much. Well, a little. It's very nice though – you should try some. Anyway, I'm not the only one who's a bit drunk – Ali is swaying around like a tree in a storm.' Meg snorts, delighted at her own turn of phrase.

'Actually, you're the one who's swaying,' says Ali, tilting to one side as she prods Meg in the chest with her empty glass.

'You both look like you're going to keel over,' Nancy says. 'Come on, let's find out where we're sitting. God, I hope Polly hasn't put me next to some deaf old aunt.' She peers over the shoulders of those already crowded around the seating plan, and calls back to tell the others they're all on table five. Meg is relieved: she had a sudden panic, just now, that Polly might have seated them separately. Not that it would have mattered, she reassures herself: she will happily chat away to whoever she ends up sitting with. She's perfectly capable of doing that anyway, but the champagne has made her feel bright and sociable to the point of invincibility. She *loves* champagne.

A large marquee has been erected at the edge of the conservatory which runs along the back of the hotel, and several sets of bifold doors have been opened and pushed back, turning it into one vast room. Meg has no idea how many people have been invited to this wedding, but there seem to be dozens of tables – all beautifully laid up with white damask tablecloths. At each place setting is an array of silver cutlery and several gleaming crystal glasses in different sizes. Instead of traditional place names, there are miniature roses for the ladies, with their names hand-written on the pots, and coasters for the men, similarly inscribed.

'Wow, this is incredible!' she says to Ali, as they move through the space, looking for table numbers. 'No expense spared.'

'You can say that again. No wonder Polly's dad looked so moody at the church – this low-key little wedding has probably bankrupted him.'

'This is us, table five!' Meg walks around until she finds her name. There is a boy/girl seating arrangement and Nancy is on the opposite side of the big round table, with Ali one seat along to Meg's left. Pulling back the chair by her place, she sinks gratefully into it; although she managed to put some plasters over the bleeding blisters on her heels when they arrived at the hotel, she can feel one of them is already working its way loose again and her squashed toe is throbbing painfully. Beneath the table she kicks off first one stiletto, then the other, gasping with relief as feeling flows back into her toes and the pressure is taken off the blisters. She has no idea how she'll manage to force her feet into them again later, but for now she doesn't care.

The table is set for ten, and a young couple are already sitting to Meg's right. She turns and smiles at them and gives a little wave, then immediately feels silly because they're right next to her. 'I'm Meg!' she says, putting her hand in her lap. 'Meg Stevens. I was at university with Polly!'

The couple look at her in surprise, then the woman smiles tightly. 'Lovely,' she says. 'So were we.' Meg feels her cheeks flushing as they both look away and begin to unfold their thick white napkins. Who are these two? There are some familiar faces here today and she has had brief conversations with several of them, but there are also many people of her own age who Meg doesn't think she has ever seen before in her life. It's possibly not surprising: Polly was always so much more sociable than she was and wherever they went at Leeds, whatever they did, she seemed to know most of the other students.

'Boring farts,' Meg mutters, picking up her own napkin and snapping it in the air to release it from its starched creases. The piece of material flies out of her hand and lands on top of the neat floral arrangement at the centre of the table, covering it like a shroud. She wants to laugh, but the man on her right has seen what happened and is shaking his head and tutting. In order to retrieve the napkin, Meg would need to stand up and lean forward as far as she can to reach the centre of the table, but she definitely can't be bothered: she has only just sat down and her feet are killing her. Instead, she swipes the napkin from the empty place setting on her other side and slips it onto her lap.

The tables around them are filling up with guests but Meg still can't see anyone she recognises. Then handsome Toby pulls out a chair on the other side of the table beside Nancy, who looks up at him and shrieks in delight. 'Hey you! This is my lucky day.'

There is still no one sitting between Ali and Meg, and the snooty couple on her other side are turned towards each other, clearly not intending to engage anyone else in conversation. To cover her embarrassment, Meg reaches for a bottle of white wine on the table in front of her, and begins to pour it into one of the crystal glasses. She isn't sure which one she's supposed to use – is the larger one meant for red or white? – but decides it doesn't really matter.

Who's going to end up sitting next to her? Please let it not be some dull middle-aged man, who will look disappointed when she says she doesn't work, then proceed to talk at her for the next three hours about his extremely important job in the City.

She leans to her left and squints at the coaster to see who has been put in the empty chair. But before she has time to read the name, a hand lands on her arm. When she turns, her heart leaps into her throat. 'Luke!' she yelps and stands up suddenly, her chair toppling over behind her, landing with a thud on the coir matting floor. The twin with the beard is grinning down at her and she moves forward to hug him, the bottle of wine still in her hand, blood roaring in her ears. 'Oh my God, it's good to see you.'

'It's Daniel,' he laughs, picking up his coaster and showing it to her.

'Daniel! Of course it is. And you've got a beard!' Meg knows she's stating the obvious, but her heart is racing and they're the only words she can manage.

He grins. 'I grew this impressive facial hair just so you could tell us apart today.'

'Oh, that's really kind of you!' she says. 'Shit, no, I didn't mean that at all. I'm such an idiot!'

'No, you're not!' He bends over to pick up her chair from the floor, before pulling out his own. 'It's good to see you again, Meg.'

She is flustered and gabbling. 'I should know which twin you are, I'm sorry! But it's been a while. Although, to be honest, I never knew if you were Luke or Daniel back in Leeds either! Do you remember that night when you made me try and guess and I got it wrong and I had to drink a pint of something, cider I think it was.'

She collapses back onto her chair, hoping her face isn't as pink as she senses it must be and willing her crazily thumping heart to calm itself. This is good, it's all good. This is the right twin. She's beside Daniel – lovely Daniel who was always so kind to her at Leeds, and so friendly. Thank God it's him and not Luke; although deep inside her a little voice is screaming out in frustration, because this is the wrong bloody twin and she would really like the man sitting beside her to be Luke.

'It's been a while, Meg,' Daniel is saying as he shuffles his chair closer to the table. 'What have you been up to?'

'Oh, this and that!' She's not sure if he really wants to know about the ins and outs of her post-university life, or whether this is just a polite conversation opener. She sets the wine bottle back onto the table in front of her. 'I live in north London now, married – to Joe, do you remember him? We were going out already in the third year – though I'm not sure if you knew each other?'

She suddenly wonders why she hadn't considered inviting the twins to her own wedding, but she'd already lost touch with so many friends from Leeds by then – even though she and Joe were only married a year after graduating. If she'd thought about it at the time – which she hadn't – it might have seemed strange to have spent three such intense years at university, feeling as if she knew some of the people there so well, but then losing touch with them again so quickly. But maybe it wasn't unusual, Joe was the same: he'd only kept in touch with his flatmates and a couple of people on his course.

'Anyway,' she says. 'We've been together ever since, and we've now got two children as well.'

'Wow!' Daniel's eyes widen, and she sees him glance down towards her stomach. 'That's great. You didn't waste any time then?'

She sucks in her belly as she replies. 'Well, it just happened,' she says. 'I mean, of course it didn't *just* happen. I did work for a while when we left uni, and Joe obviously works.' She feels her face flush again; what a stupid thing to say – of course Joe works! 'But we both knew we wanted a family, so there didn't seem much point in waiting, and I liked my job but it wasn't *the* most important thing in my life. I've never thought a career has to define you.'

She's babbling again and covers up her awkwardness by taking another sip of wine. Why does she always feel the need to justify herself like this? There was a baby crying in the church during the ceremony itself, but she hasn't seen it here at the hotel, and there aren't any guests who appear to have a small child in tow, so Polly and Adam have probably made their reception child-free, which is understandable. But that doesn't mean there aren't other parents here, quite possibly some of those who are a similar age to her and were students alongside them all at Leeds. It's not as if she's a total freak for getting pregnant in her early twenties.

She puts her wine glass back on the table and drops her hands onto her lap, automatically holding them across her dress to disguise the bulge. Daniel hadn't meant to glance down at her stomach, it was a subconscious reaction to what she was saying about having children, but it makes Meg want to bring up the subject again, remind him there's a reason for the way she looks:

I'm a mother, a parent, I've been pregnant – I didn't choose to be like this, I'm not just greedy or lazy. This body has given birth to two babies! The need to defend herself is overpowering but, even with several glasses of champagne inside her, she knows now is not the time to have that kind of conversation.

'I can't say I'm impressed by whoever laid this table,' Daniel is saying. 'Since when did napkins go on top of the flower arrangements?' He leans forward and pulls the white napkin onto his lap. 'I see you've started on the wine. Feel like pouring some of it into my glass?'

'Yes! Of course.' She grabs at the bottle too quickly and her fingers slip off the neck, causing it to spin to one side. Daniel's hand reaches out just in time to steady it and stop the contents flooding across the tablecloth.

'Hey, careful!' he grins. 'Looks like you're no better at holding your booze now, than you were at Leeds all those years ago.'

Meg laughs. 'I don't get to indulge much nowadays.' She knows he's making fun of her, but doesn't care.

CHAPTER NINE

The speeches are great. Meg hasn't been to many weddings, but at most of the ones she has attended, she found herself laughing politely at appropriate moments and clapping with relief when whoever was standing up at the top table, finished doing their bit and collapsed back down into a chair. Some wedding speeches were moving, others witty, but the majority fell somewhere in between and invariably went on for too long.

At her own wedding, she'd wanted the dance floor to open up and swallow her when Joe's best man – whom they both loved dearly – muddled his way through a speech that would have been dull at half the length. He'd had far too much lager to steady his nerves and laughed so much at what he'd written on the scraps of paper in his hands, that no one else could understand what he was saying. It was just as well: her parents wouldn't have appreciated the story about the gorilla suit and the bag of weed.

As she listens to today's best man recount bawdy stories about Adam, Meg watches Polly's parents. They're clearly drunk and enjoying themselves: her father is leaning back in his chair looking relaxed and laughing. Polly's mother's hat is askew and she looks happy and pretty, an older, slightly more rounded version of her daughters.

Many years ago, Meg met this couple when she was one of a small group of rowdy students who decamped to Polly's family home for a weekend, but she doesn't remember much about the visit, let alone about Polly's parents, and there's no way they'd remember anything about her.

On the other side of the top table, Adam's mother is sitting with pursed lips, looking as if someone nearby has farted. She hasn't cracked a smile at any of the best man's jokes – even the ones that aren't about her darling boy – and is clearly hoping this hellish experience will be over as quickly as possible.

Meg wonders what sort of a mother-in-law she'll make for Polly: not a particularly easy one, if the comment that bloke made earlier is anything to go by. While they were all still swilling champagne and looking for an opportunity to grab another bite-size canapé, she overheard someone say that Adam is an only child and his father died several years ago, so it wouldn't be surprising if his mother is struggling with this wedding. It must be sad to have to sit here and be part of so much happiness and cheer, without being able to share it all with her husband.

Adam's mother will also know that the point of these celebrations is to send her son off on the next stage of his life. This ceremony is to mark the fact that she's losing her boy to another woman. That must be hard for any mother and Meg can't imagine how she'll feel in twenty or thirty years' time, when Ollie gets married.

She hopes she'll be a kind, approachable mother-in-law, sharing jokes with whoever her son marries, telling stories about the chaos he caused when he was young. The sort of mother-in-law who offers support, but never demands to be included and consulted. Judging by the grim expression on Adam's mother's face, it doesn't look as if there's huge potential for a mutually beneficial relationship for Polly.

Meg's own experiences in that department haven't been great. Joe's mother, Anne, has never thought Meg was good enough for her boy; she hasn't said as much to either of them, but she doesn't need to. Meg doesn't miss the looks Anne gives her when Ollie is throwing a tantrum or Tallulah's refusing to eat her tea. She catches the occasional eye roll when Meg herself says something Anne disagrees with; knowing her mother-in-law has such a low opinion of her, makes her nervous in the woman's company, constantly on edge and worried about her own behaviour, let alone that of her loud, stubborn, occasionally naughty small children.

Ironically, this means Meg frequently comes out with remarks that sound stupid, even to her own ears. Jokes that fall flat, or comments about something they've both just watched on television; the harder Meg tries to be witty, clever – or just vaguely interesting – the more strained and awkward her words sound. Feeling judged is horrible.

Meg has talked to Joe about this, but he tells her she's being paranoid. 'Mum's really fond of you! She's always saying how lucky she is to have such a wonderful daughter-in-law.' Meg doesn't believe him, but loves him too much to make a crisis out of what is – most of the time – no more than an irritation. Anne lives in the Lake District, so only comes to stay for two or three days every few months and, although those visits are a struggle, Meg works hard to ensure they go smoothly. She is – as Nancy reminded her only an hour or so ago – a natural born peacekeeper.

Everyone at the table around her starts cheering and raising glasses, and Meg reaches for her own glass, realising the best man has finally finished ripping Adam's reputation to shreds and is now toasting the bridesmaids or the happy couple or whoever else has yet to be mentioned at the top table.

As the guests settle down again, Polly surprises no one by insisting she wants to speak as well. 'I know it's not traditional,' she says, as she stands up. 'But nor am I!'

Laughter ripples around the room and a woman over the other side yells, 'We wouldn't want you any other way!'

Polly wriggles a little to adjust her dress and takes a sip of wine, before putting her hand onto Adam's shoulder. 'I just want to tell you all, how special it is to have you here today,' she begins. 'It means so much to both of us.' Adam nods and puts his hand on top of hers. 'You'll be relieved to hear,' she continues. 'That I'm going to make this quick...'

'Thank God for that!' someone calls out.

'...but I just want to say some personal thank-yous and mention a few people who have worked so hard to make today go smoothly.'

Meg watches as her friend holds the attention of the room. Polly never had any qualms about public speaking. At Leeds, she joined the drama society in the first term and invited Meg to go to a performance they put on before Christmas. At that stage they didn't know each other very well, but Meg was grateful to have been singled out by this clever, pretty, witty girl. They often sat next to each other in English lectures and were in the same tutorial group, and Meg – never confident about the space she occupied in a roomful of virtual strangers – basked in Polly's generous shadow.

The play was dire – it was a ghost story written by the third-year drama student who ran the society and was fully expecting to be the next Kate Winslet – but Polly was great, and the invitation cemented their friendship.

From then on, Meg found herself swept into Polly's inner circle. She met Ali almost immediately – she and Polly had rooms next door to each other in the same student flat – and the three of them moved into a house together in the second year, along with a girl called Danni, who was fun and friendly but never a major part of their lives because she ended up spending most of the time at her boyfriend's.

Although Polly had brought Nancy into their little group during that second year, Meg now found it hard to remember what it had been like before that, when it was just the three of them. That was possibly because Nancy had always been such a forceful character, but Meg suspected it was also because, during that first year, she had constantly felt as if she was finding her feet. So much about university life was different and exciting – and at times unnerving and confusing – but while it was happening, Meg hadn't been aware of quite how hard she was working to fit in and establish herself in this new environment.

By the time the second year came around, she was more comfortable in her own skin. She was never sure if the others felt the same about those early days – possibly not: Ali and Polly seemed to ooze effortless self-confidence – but Meg gradually came to feel more relaxed, and stopped worrying quite so much about having to prove herself.

But there's no doubt, she thinks now, looking at her friend standing up in front of a crowd of a hundred of her close friends and family, that Polly has always been the glue that held them together. In their different ways, Meg, Ali and Nancy were all keen to claim her as their best friend back then. As her flatmate from the day they arrived at uni, Ali seemed to have a head start in the friendship stakes. But Meg loved having Polly to herself in lectures and seminars, and they spent a lot of time together in the library – sometimes working, more often chatting and time-wasting.

Then, after they all graduated, Polly and Nancy went

travelling, spending six months in the States and South America. When they came back, Polly started her graduate consultancy internship and Nancy went into teacher training.

By that time, Ali had already begun to make her mark in engineering and Meg happily trotted along beside them all. Her first job after she left Leeds, ended up being her only job: running the social media accounts and marketing for a small recruitment company in north London. Even at the time, it wasn't what she wanted to be doing for the rest of her life, but it paid an almost decent salary. Anyway, by then she had Joe – her boyfriend since the final year – and her trajectory was always going to be different to that of her successful friends.

'Meg, you're just the loveliest person,' Ali once said to her. 'I don't know anyone who's quite as sweet and funny as you.' Meg suspected there was some unspoken acknowledgement in there: that her sweet, funny personality was seen as recompense for the fact that she wasn't as high powered as the rest of them. But if that was the case, it wasn't meant to be hurtful; she knew Ali respected her decision to step off the career conveyor belt and start a family. Anyway, Meg was sure she was just being paranoid, as usual.

As she holds the floor at her own wedding, Polly is speaking without notes, mentioning her parents and her sister, thanking her new mother-in-law for her help with the flowers and telling a funny story about one of the ushers who drove down from Manchester yesterday without the morning suit he'd hired, so had to pay twice as much as the original hire fee, to get it couriered down late last night. The man in question stands up and takes a mock bow as the guests cheer and applaud.

'Adam and I are thrilled to see so many of our friends here,' Polly says. 'From school and university, from work. You've come from as far away as Sweden, Italy and New Zealand to be with us.'

'And Brighton!' yells a man behind Meg.

'Yes, even Brighton!' Polly laughs. 'But thank you all, whether you've come eleven or 11,000 miles. We feel blessed to be surrounded by so many wonderful human beings.' She's smiling as she looks around the room and that smile broadens and her head tips slightly to one side as her eyes land on one of the tables nearest to her, clearly seeing someone special.

Meg cranes her neck to one side, trying to spot who it is. But there are too many tables in between; too many heads blocking her view.

CHAPTER TEN

The little photographer is back in action, leaping in and out between the round tables, taking what he hopes will be candid snaps of the guests as they chat and drink and relax. He is suddenly leaning down on the opposite side of the table, almost pushing Nancy to one side as he points his lens at Meg and Daniel. The central flower display is in the way, but Meg guesses that's the point. If her face features in the final shot at all, it will be as softened background, carefully draped in feathery green foliage.

'More wine?' asks Daniel. The applause has died away after Polly's speech and she is now sitting back down at the top table, her arms draped around her new husband. 'That glass is empty again.'

'I really shouldn't,' Meg says. When she first sat down at the table at the start of the meal, she was already drunk, her stomach churning and the room occasionally spinning at the edges when she turned her head too quickly to talk to Daniel. But eating has helped – there were three courses, all of them substantial and delicious – and she not only ate what was on her own plate, but finished off Ali's pudding. As usual, her friend only picked at her food and, when she pushed her bowl away, Meg leant across and grabbed it, unable to resist a second helping of the delicately arranged trio of strawberry shortbread trifle, peanut butter cupcake and chocolate and coconut cookie. 'Oh wow, this is *amazing!*' she grinned at Daniel, as she ran her spoon around the bowl to scrape up the remnants.

She now feels so stuffed, she doesn't think she can move, but at least all the food will have soaked up some of the alcohol. Anyway, waiters are streaming through the marquee carrying coffee pots and milk jugs, so there's no harm in having a top up if she washes it down with caffeine. She smiles at Daniel. 'Go on then,' she grins. 'Just one more glass.'

He pours out some wine, but then sees there's hardly anything left in the bottle, so moves it forward again and tops up her glass to the brim. 'Come on Meg!' he laughs, as she tuts and tries to cover the top of the glass with her hand. 'Let your hair down.'

She isn't the only one who has already had a skinful. On the other side of Daniel, Ali pushes back her chair and staggers to her feet. Meg can't remember ever seeing her this pissed – even when they were nineteen-year-old students who hadn't had much practice at holding their drink. Ali sways backwards before grabbing the table to steady herself. 'Off for a wee!' she announces, before turning and teetering away towards the far end of the marquee.

To Meg's right, the couple from Leeds are still ignoring her. Neither has turned in her direction throughout the entire meal. Meg wants to knock her glass of wine over the man's expensive shiny suit: really childish, but she doesn't care. Yet more snotty people judging her. What right do they have to pretend she doesn't exist? Sod them.

'So, Dan,' she says. 'Daniel. Dan. Can I call you that?'

He is grinning at her. 'Meg, dear Meg. You can call me whatever you want.'

'Good. Then I will call you Dan. Did I call you that at Leeds?' She honestly can't remember. 'What did you think of me? Back then?'

He is leaning forward, elbows on the table, nursing a glass of red wine, possibly nearly as drunk as she is. 'Hah! What a question. Well, you were always funny Meg – I remember Luke saying you should have a go at stand-up. Do you remember that comedy night they had once a month at the student union?'

Meg remembers it very well. She'd enjoyed finding she could make people laugh when she went to university, but it had only been on a small scale: stand-up felt like a giant step too far. She had batted away calls from her friends to take part in the regular comedy free-for-all, but then sat amongst the heckling audience, wishing she'd had a go, convinced she could do better than whichever student was standing up in front of them all, bumbling on about drugs or sex or some other equally obvious and overdone topic.

'Did he?' she says now. 'Did Luke say that?' It felt important, somehow, that he'd thought she was witty enough to do stand-up. Or just that she had the balls to do it. 'I'm not sure I'm particularly funny anymore.'

'You were also very sweet!' Daniel adds.

Oh God, that bloody word again. She hates it. 'That's what Ali always used to say to me! It's so boring! Sweet is nothing. It's harmless and pathetic. I don't want to be *sweet*.'

Dan snorts and takes a sip of his wine. 'Nothing wrong with sweet, Meg. You could have been a lot worse. Ali probably said that because...'

She waits for him to go on, but he turns his head away towards a commotion at the far end of the marquee.

'They're cutting the cake!' someone calls from behind her.

Around them, guests begin to cheer; Polly and Adam have left the top table and are making their way towards a small table in the corner of the marquee, on which stands a sumptuous three-tier cake, decorated with a profusion of pressed flowers.

The photographer is leaping about, guests are applauding and Adam is standing behind Polly, wrapping his arms around her waist as they both hold a knife against the frosted white icing.

Meg presumes she and Joe must have had pictures taken of their own cake cutting, but bizarrely she can't now recall either cutting their traditional fruitcake or seeing the photographic evidence. But they will undoubtedly be among the 120 images in their embossed wedding album, which is on the bottom shelf beside the TV. It's been a while since either of them got it out to look through it – years actually, since way before Tallulah was born. Maybe Nancy is right about all this excessive wedding craziness.

As waiters begin to distribute slices of cake on small plates, Meg turns back to Daniel. 'What were you going to say, about Ali?'

He is leaning his elbows on the table, hunched over his wine glass, and looks at her in confusion. 'Sorry?'

'Ali Benson! The Ali who's been sitting next to you! You were saying how she used to tell me I was sweet.'

Comprehension dawns. 'Oh yes! I just thought Ali said that to you because she was hitting on you.'

Meg's mouth drops open. 'She never hit on me!'

Daniel shrugs. 'No? Oh well, don't take it personally. You probably weren't her type.'

Meg stares at him, lost for words. 'That's not what I meant. I just...'

Suddenly an arm wraps itself around her, grabbing her shoulder, and she feels the weight of a head pressing against her cheek. 'Megster!' Luke's breath is wine-infused, his skin – lacking a beard to match that of his twin – surprisingly soft. 'How are you? I saw Dan had lucked out in sitting next to you. You're looking as gorgeous as ever.'

The breath has gone out of her body, as if she's been kicked in the guts. His arm feels so strong around her and she grabs it, steadying herself. 'Luke! Hi! Hey, good to see you. How are you?'

But he's already speaking to his brother. 'Dan, there's that bloke at my table who did the resourcing at Donaldsons. You know, the one Adam recommended? Come over and I'll introduce you. I know you aren't meant to talk shop at weddings, but at least if you swap numbers, you can contact him next week.'

There's a scraping sound as Daniel pushes back his chair and throws his napkin down at his place setting and, before Meg has a chance to say anything, they're both gone, wending their way through chairs to the other side of the room.

Meg watches them go, deafened by the thud of her own heartbeat. When she turns back to the table, she realises the man on her right is finally looking at her. She smiles brightly and raises her glass, which Daniel filled almost to the brim. 'Cheers!' she says. She decides she really ought to make an effort with this miserable couple, so tries to read the name inscribed on the coaster in front of him. Bernie something. Bernie White? Waite? She screws up her eyes and leans forward, concentrating so hard on trying to make out the lettering that she doesn't notice she's spilling her wine until the liquid starts to drip onto her wrist. As she jerks upright, she feels a hand on her shoulder.

'Hello, everyone! How was the meal?'

For the first time since they all sat down, the couple beside her smile; they and all the other guests are looking up at whoever is standing right behind Meg.

'Polly!' she exclaims, leaning backwards so suddenly that the room does a quick flip around her. 'There you are!'

'Darling Meg, are you having a good time?'

She doesn't have a chance to answer, because the bride is already working the table, smiling around at them all, waving to Nancy on the opposite side, taking her hand off Meg's shoulder and moving it onto the forearm of the man beside her.

'Bernie, how was New York, I hear you're opening a new office over there? Eleanor, your dress is fantastic – and I saw you wearing that gorgeous hat outside the church! Did you get your photo taken with Alex? I'll need to get a copy of that one.'

Polly always knew how to do this sort of thing. As well as performing in plays at Leeds, she joined the debating society and the girls went along to support her on several occasions.

There was one debate, against a team from Sheffield Uni, where Polly proposed the motion that all social media should be banned for anyone under the age of eighteen. Those in the hall were only a year or two older than that, and most started out by disagreeing with her, but she won the debate. When Meg congratulated her afterwards, Polly winked at her and whispered, 'That was such a load of bollocks – I can't believe they fell for it!'

All these years later, at her own wedding, she is still oozing the charm that has always served her so well. She does it effortlessly, throwing out first names, slipping little personal nuggets into her greetings. Meg envies the way she can juggle them all like this, making every single one of her guests feel special and as if they're playing a vitally important part in her big day. She glides around the table, saying hello, bending over to kiss proffered cheeks, accepting compliments on her dress. Despite the fact that they are several hours into this wedding and Polly has probably been up since dawn getting ready, she looks as fresh as she did when Meg saw her stepping out of the Rolls Royce outside the church.

Adam has skipped their table and is at the one beside it, doing a similar walkabout: patting shoulders, shaking hands, kissing more cheeks. The bride and groom double act is clearly something that has been planned for this stage in the proceedings and Meg remembers her own mother sending her off from the top table to make sure all the guests were having a good time. 'Go and say hello to Uncle Donald and Aunty Margaret,' she'd insisted. 'They've come all the way from Glasgow and they'll expect a thank you for their present.'

After all these years, Meg has no idea what that present might have been, and she doubts she did the bridal schmoozing nearly as well as Polly is doing it now. Although it's not really schmoozing, because this couple have no need to impress any of the people in this room. They are the deserving stars of their own show and nothing and nobody can eclipse the spotlight shining on them today.

'Pol!' Meg calls out, lifting up her hand and trying to attract the bride's attention. That quick hello wasn't enough – she wants to give Polly a hug and have a proper conversation with her; she wants to tell her how beautiful she looks and how much she appreciates being invited here to celebrate with them. She wants everyone else around this table to see them together and realise how close they are, and how much this beautiful bride loves and appreciates her dear friend, Meg.

But Polly and Adam have both turned away and are now at the next two tables. Somehow, they crossed over on the way and Polly is standing by the table that's furthest away, her hand resting on the back of a chair as she starts the process all over again. 'Wasn't the beef delicious?' she is saying to a woman dressed in bright green.

Meg lowers her own hand and picks up her wine glass to cover her embarrassment. Polly didn't ignore her; she just didn't hear her call out. There are so many people here today, so many friends and family who want to share this celebration and witness her happiness – it's not surprising she isn't able to have a proper catch-up with everyone. Meg takes another swig of white wine and leans back in her chair; she will see Polly later: there are hours and hours of this wedding still to come.

The newly-weds have now met again on the other side of the tables and are heading towards the far end of the room, their hands clasped. Adam turns and pulls Polly gently towards him, kissing her quickly on the cheek before they carry on walking. Meg thinks she might cry; bloody hell, these two will make some beautiful children. She wonders if they'll try for a baby straight away or enjoy a year or two of married life first.

Polly's career is clearly important to her, but surely she'll want to start a family at some stage. Strangely, they've never had this conversation. Over the last few years, Polly has come to see Meg after the babies were born, and done the right things and made all the right noises, but she has never seemed particularly broody. That's probably because she's still got so much time: she may be nearly thirty, but nowadays that isn't old when it comes to getting pregnant.

There's a screech from the other side of the table, and Nancy throws her head back and laughs so loudly that people nearby turn to see what's going on. Her hand is on top of Toby's on the table, and she has her other arm draped around his shoulders, her fingers resting on his neck, just above his collar. Meg watches, fascinated: it's such an intimate gesture. Their faces are turned towards each other, so close their cheeks are almost touching. Did he come with anyone today? If so, whoever it was, appears to have lost him to Nancy.

And what about Jeff? She's never particularly liked him but

Meg now feels sorry for him: thank God he isn't here to see his girlfriend throwing herself at Toby. Nancy has always been a flirt, but today she's going in all guns blazing. As Meg stares at them through the central flower arrangement, Nancy looks up suddenly. There's no time for Meg to turn away, and she sees something harden in Nancy's expression, her eyes widening ever so slightly in an acknowledgement that's far from friendly. She may as well be yelling, *what the hell are you looking at?* Then she turns back to Toby and says something to him, her lips millimetres from his ear.

Meg looks away quickly, feeling guilty, though she's not the one who has anything to feel bad about. Beside her, Bernie White or Waite puts his napkin on the table, pushes back his chair and gets up. As he walks away, Meg leans towards his other half – who she now knows is called Eleanor – hoping to make polite conversation, but the woman ignores her and looks down at her phone. The gaps left by the two empty chairs on either side of Meg now feel very large indeed. She leans forward and grabs the bottle in front of her. More wine is called for.

CHAPTER ELEVEN

A li weaves her way back from the ladies and throws herself down into the chair beside Meg. Cups and saucers have appeared in front of them and waiters have swiftly and efficiently filled them with coffee.

On the other side of the table, Toby pushes back his chair and gets up. 'Don't go!' Nancy is wailing at him. 'Don't leave me!' They are both laughing and he eventually pulls himself out of her grasp and heads off towards the entrance.

'Come and sit by us,' Ali says, patting the empty chair beside her. 'You look all lonely over there.'

Nancy doesn't seem thrilled by the idea, but moves around the table and joins them.

'You haven't touched your coffee,' Ali says. 'That's not like you.'

Nancy shrugs. 'Just not feeling like it today.'

'But you *love* your coffee, Nance! You always say you can't function until you've had three cups of bulletproof espresso!'

'Well, I'm trying to be more healthy, okay?' Nancy snaps. 'Cutting back on caffeine.'

'Wow,' Ali says. 'I never expected that from you, of all

people. When we were in Lisbon for that weekend last year, you made us seek out that really famous coffee shop, do you remember? The one where they roasted their own beans and sold them in those tiny hessian bags!'

Meg notices how pale Nancy is. There are dark bags under her eyes and she looks drawn, which is strange because she hasn't drunk much alcohol today. In fact, she hasn't seemed to be drinking at all.

'I would have thought hell would freeze over before you gave up coffee,' Ali carries on. 'You're the only person I know who cares so much about her fancy coffee blend that she buys it direct from an importer!'

There are some small dark blotches around Nancy's eyes. Meg hasn't noticed them before, probably because she wasn't looking for them. She is looking now though. Those blotches are familiar: Meg's skin looked the same – both times.

'Nancy,' she says, leaning forward. 'Tell me to mind my own business, but... are you?'

'Is she what?' asks Ali.

Nancy looks at Meg for a couple of seconds, then nods.

'Oh my God!' Meg clasps her hand across her mouth. 'Nancy! That's amazing!'

'What's amazing?' Ali leans forward, frowning. 'Sorry, but what am I missing?'

Nancy turns to Ali. 'I'm pregnant.'

Ali gasps. 'What?'

'Pregnant. You know: expecting, with child, up the duff, bun in the oven.'

'I know what pregnant means! But... fuck! Oh my God, Nance, it's just a shock! Why didn't you tell us? Congratulations. Bloody hell, this is not something I ever expected to hear. Well, I don't mean ever, but not right now. Was it planned? How does Jeff feel about it?'

Nancy is putting her hands over her ears. 'Enough, Ali! For God's sake, calm down, one thing at a time. No, it wasn't planned, and yes it was as much of a shock to me as it clearly is to you.'

'Well, I think it's wonderful,' says Meg. She reaches across the table, but Nancy pulls her hand away and puts in on her lap. 'I'm so pleased for you. Why didn't you tell us before?'

'It's early days,' Nancy says. 'I wasn't going to tell you at all. I'd much rather have kept it to myself. But I did think you might pick up on the fact that I wasn't drinking.'

'We would have done, if we hadn't been so busy getting pissed ourselves,' Ali laughs. 'But you have to admit, it is a surprise, Nance. I mean, you've never seemed like the sort of person who was in a hurry to settle down and have babies. Your career has always been really important to you. You're doing so well at school, what with being head of the English department now and everything.'

Meg agrees. She has always assumed Nancy doesn't want children, despite choosing to spend the majority of every weekday surrounded by them. Or possibly because of that. Ever since she entered education and started to spend much of her time in classrooms, she has been so cynical, not only about children, but about parents and parenting.

Nancy was never one of those friends who rushed to visit after the birth of a baby, bearing a cute Babygro and begging to hold the new arrival. She didn't come to see Ollie until he was nearly a month old, and then she said she wasn't bothered about holding him and sat on the far end of the sofa, quickly changing the conversation away from sore nipples and nappy explosions, back to work and whatever was happening in the outside world. It had upset Meg at the time, because all she wanted to do was show off her adored newborn to her closest friends. But she told herself this was just Nancy; she wasn't the maternal type.

'I won't be giving up my job,' she says now. 'I'll be going back to work as soon as I possibly can. Haven't thought through the logistics yet, but I'll sort it all somehow.'

Meg suspects there's a subliminal criticism of her own life choices lurking in there, if she chooses to take it that way. But she doesn't. 'I can't imagine you not going back to work,' she says. 'Your career is so important to you, so I'm sure you'll sort things out. Will Jeff be eligible for paternity leave? You might be able to dovetail your time off. Or maybe the school will let you go back part time at first?'

Nancy shrugs. 'Possibly. But Jeff isn't in the picture, so that lessens the options.'

Ali and Meg both stare at her.

'You've split up?' Ali asks.

Nancy nods.

'Yet another major life event which you chose to keep to yourself!' Ali says. 'When did that happen? I thought things had got better between you?'

'It's been on and off for a while,' Nancy says. 'But we officially split two months ago and he moved out.'

'But he'll stand by you?' Ali's brow is furrowed with concern. 'I mean, he won't let you go through all this on your own?'

'As I just *told* you,' Nancy says. 'He won't be in the picture.'

Ali's mouth drops open. 'But... I can't imagine Jeff doing that, walking away from you. He's a nice guy, far too steady.'

'He doesn't know I'm pregnant.'

'But when you do tell him,' Meg says, 'obviously he'll want to be involved?'

'He won't be bringing up this child with me.' Nancy glares at her, a muscle twitching underneath her left eye.

'What do you mean?'

'I mean that, at some stage, I will tell him I'm pregnant. But there's no rush for me to do that, because it's not his baby.'

The other two stare at her. There's an obvious question that hangs in the air between the three of them, but Meg hasn't got the nerve to ask it, and it doesn't seem as if Ali has either.

'Anyway,' Nancy continues. 'I had no intention of breaking this news to you today, so can we move on from the subject for the time being? We're here to celebrate Polly's big day, not discuss my future.'

She clearly wants to shut down the conversation, but there's so much more Meg wants to ask, so many things she wants to talk about. If this was any other of her friends, they would already be discussing due dates and maternity leave, she'd be sympathising about morning sickness and recommending ginger biscuits and herbal tea. If this was any other of her friends, Meg would also feel able to ask the most important question: who's the father?

She doesn't know Jeff very well, so isn't particularly affected either way by the news that he and Nancy aren't together anymore. But if Jeff isn't the father of this baby, then who is? Has Nancy been seeing someone else properly or did she just have a brief – presumably rather careless – fling?

Meg's mind is racing as she weighs up the possibilities and, looking across the table, she catches Ali's eye. They are both clearly desperate to ask more questions, but they know Nancy well enough to realise that, right now, pushing her for more information would be a mistake.

'Wow,' Ali says. 'Well, congratulations. I guess. Are you happy about all this?'

Nancy shrugs. 'Happy isn't the right word. But I'm keeping it – if that's what you mean.'

Meg had felt so different when she discovered she was pregnant: from the moment she saw the little blue line appear on the pregnancy test, she'd wanted to shout it out to the world, send texts to everyone in her contacts list.

She was so excited and happy, she would have shared the news with strangers in the corner shop or posted it on Instagram, TikTok and every other form of social media. Joe had been the one to urge restraint until they'd reached the perceived safety of twelve weeks and, although Meg had reluctantly agreed it was sensible to keep quiet, once that first trimester was over, she told everyone she met within the first thirty seconds, including the elderly couple who live next door, the car insurance call centre agent and the man who came to service the boiler.

But Meg can understand Nancy's reticence. This is such a major life event and the consequences of it are so far-reaching. Meg isn't sure she would have been so blissfully ecstatic to be pregnant if she hadn't had a supportive partner and been able to relax and enjoy her pregnancy in the knowledge that she didn't need to go back to work and earn money. For Nancy, this is going to be a totally different experience, and not necessarily an easy one.

'And just so you know,' Nancy says. 'I told Polly last weekend when we went out for lunch. So, you don't need to worry about keeping the news from her.'

'Okay,' Ali nods. 'Well, that's good.'

Meg puts her napkin down on the table and folds it into a neat square. She realises she's envious of Nancy, starting this journey. She would give anything to turn back the clock and have Ollie and Tallulah as babies again. It was such a beautiful stage; they were so tiny and defenceless, totally dependent, needing her more than anyone else in the world.

Having said that, it was also hard work and relentless and the lack of sleep was a grind. Meg struggled with breast feeding – yet another thing that everyone raved about and said should come naturally – but for her it was painful and stressful.

Although she stopped feeding Tallulah eighteen months ago, she still vividly recalls the sharp sting as the baby took her nipple in its mouth and sucked with a strength that seemed incredible for one so tiny. Now, of course, with some of the harder parts of pregnancy and new motherhood just a distant memory, she can cheerfully claim it was all worth it: the exhaustion, the stretchmarks, the saggy belly and the weight gain. Despite what it did to her body – and occasionally to her mind – being pregnant, giving birth and raising her babies is the most wonderful thing that has ever happened to her.

And now Nancy is going to go through all of that, and Meg is jealous, because her own children are little people with personalities and actual lives of their own, and they don't need her in the same all-consuming way they did during those first few months of life. Ollie, her adored firstborn, doesn't seem to need her at all, but that's something she really doesn't want to dwell on right now. Her heart flips as she thinks of him, a dart of panic taking her away from this table and back to her little house in north London. She takes a deep breath and smiles at Nancy, who doesn't acknowledge it because she's staring down, playing with her cutlery, her expression far from happy.

'It will be wonderful,' Meg says. She gets up from her chair and goes to Nancy, staggering a little as she does – realising how drunk she is, now she's standing up. Nancy's shoulders are stiff and, at first, she doesn't react to the hug.

But as Meg refuses to let go, she feels her friend's body soften and relax, and Nancy looks up at her and nods, gives her a small smile. 'You are so lucky,' whispers Meg.

CHAPTER TWELVE

As Meg pushes open the door into the ladies' cloakroom, her mobile rings. Fumbling to pull it from her bag, she staggers against the wall-mounted hand-dryer and the phone flies out of her hand, clattering onto the tiled floor. She bends to pick it up, but the room begins to spin around her and suddenly she finds herself on her hands and knees, grappling for the handset as it shoots across the floor, through the feet of two women who are walking out past her, one of them snorting with laughter.

'You alright?' the other asks, leaning down towards her.

'Yes, I'm fine!' Meg says. 'Totally fine!'

As the door slams after them, she hears their shrieks. 'Bloody hell! Did you see the state of her?'

The phone is still ringing.

'Shit, shit,' she mutters, pulling it towards her and jabbing frantically at the screen. After what seems like hours, it lights up and she sees Joe's name.

'What?' she says, sitting back on her heels. 'What is it?'

There's a voice on the other end, but it's so distant she can't make out what it's saying. 'Joe? What's happened?' She holds the phone away from her ear and realises it's upside down. The room has stopped spinning, but she's breathing so heavily she can still hardly hear his voice over the thumping of her own heart.

'Nothing!' Joe's laughing. 'Just thought we'd give you a call, didn't we, kids? See how Mummy's getting on.'

Meg's head starts to throb and she turns and lets her legs slide out in front of her, leaning against the wall, the red and grey flock wallpaper reassuringly soft against the back of her head. She has now been in here several times today – she has lost count of exactly how many times – but reckons she has gone through nearly half a bottle of the Molton Brown hand cream – at least she's getting her money's worth from this expensive hotel. The thought makes her snort with laughter.

'So, how's it going?' Joe is asking. 'Lula! Do you want to speak to Mummy?' There's shouting in the background, something clattering.

'Why are you home so early?' Meg asks. She hears herself slurring and takes a deep breath. 'I thought they were going on playdates after school?'

'They did! It's nearly six o'clock, so we've been home for an hour or so, had tea – that lasagna was really good, by the way – and now it's bath time, so I thought we'd give you a ring before we go upstairs.'

Meg closes her eyes and can picture them as he speaks: Joe will be standing in the kitchen surrounded by unpacked school bags and lunchboxes, the dirty plates and cutlery from dinner still on the kitchen table. Ollie will have run off into the other room to turn on the television – knowing his dad isn't nearly as firm about that kind of thing as Meg – and Tallulah is probably still strapped into the little booster seat they keep on a chair at the kitchen table, with tomato sauce from the lasagna smeared across her cheeks and through her hair. If Joe doesn't get her out soon, she'll start mashing bits of food into the table with her fingers before wiping them across the front of her T-shirt.

'Ollie?' Joe's calling now. 'Come and say hello to Mummy on the phone!'

Meg thinks back to the clothes she laid out for Tallulah to wear today: she'd chosen that pretty pale pink T-shirt, the Boden one Joe's mother bought for her. Tomato sauce is a bugger to get out at the best of times, it will be even worse by the time she gets home tomorrow and tries to deal with it. This is bloody typical. She has only been away for half a day and things have already descended into chaos. Is it really six o'clock? God knows where the last few hours have gone. They were eating for a while and there were lots of speeches, but if anyone had asked Meg the time, she'd wouldn't have guessed it was nearly that late.

'What's she doing?' she asks, her head resting on her free hand. 'Tallulah, I mean, what's she doing? I bet she's making a mess. If that's really the time, why aren't they in the bath already? For God's sake, Joe – I know it's Friday, but they still need to stick to a routine. I bet Ollie's stuck in front of the TV as well, isn't he? There are no kids programmes on at this time of night, he's probably watching something completely unsuitable.'

She imagines her five-year-old son using the remote to flick through channels, images from the early evening news flashing in front of him: crying children, bombed-out cities, refugees drowning in the Channel. Sometimes she can't even bear to watch the news herself and there's no way she ever lets Ollie anywhere near it. By this age he should be old enough to have some comprehension of right and wrong, yet it scares her that he still seems unable to translate that to his own behaviour. Watching violence and aggression played out on the TV screen in their sitting room isn't going to help matters.

'No, he's not watching television,' Joe says. 'I told him he could go and find a DVD...'

'Well, he shouldn't be doing that! He always manages to twist you round his little finger. Honestly!'

'Why can't he watch a DVD? They're all bloody Pixar or whatever, it's not as if we've got a secret porn collection stashed away. Why are you making a big deal out of it?'

'Because Ollie knows exactly how to get what he wants out of you, because you've never got your eye on the ball.' Meg isn't quite sure why she's yelling, but she's pissed off with Joe for not having Ollie right there beside him, where he can see what he's getting up to. But she can't say that, because it sounds insane.

She opens her eyes and stares at the wall on the other side of the room, her head starting to spin again as her eyes trace the red and grey floral pattern on the wallpaper, fronds of something slightly other-worldly twisting their way towards the ceiling.

There's silence on the other end of the phone and she closes her eyes again to block out the spinning. 'Are you listening to me, Joe?'

When he answers, he seems bemused. 'Meg are you okay? You sound odd. Look, I'm really sorry I called – I shouldn't have bothered you. I just thought you'd want to speak to the kids, maybe say goodnight or whatever. But I didn't think it through, of course you're tied up. Don't worry, everything's fine here, really. You don't need to be worrying about us, I want you to have a good time.'

'I *am* having a good time! Or I was, until you called. I wasn't even worrying – why would I worry? You're their bloody father, Joe, I should be able to leave the kids with you without having to consider any of you. I should just be able to be here – wherever the fuck here is, Wales somewhere, I don't know – without having you call to check up on me.'

'Meg, that's ridiculous – and bloody unfair. I'm not checking up on you.' She can hear the hurt in his voice. 'The kids and I were just talking about you and I thought it would be nice to see how you were and let them say hello to you.'

She knows this, and she knows she is being totally unreasonable. But for some reason she can't step away from this ridiculous conversation. 'Well, I'm going to see you all tomorrow! It's not as if I'm away for a week.'

The door beside Meg's feet swings open and a middle-aged woman walks into the ladies. 'Oh, sorry!' she mock-whispers, putting her finger to her lips and tiptoeing in exaggerated, drunken steps over Meg's outstretched legs towards a cubicle.

Meg closes her eyes again, holding the phone to her ear. She ought to say sorry. None of this is going the right way – why did she start yelling at Joe? She isn't actually sure and can't remember how it started; things are going all wrong and she has no idea if this is her fault or his, but is pretty sure it's hers.

'It's just... why do you need to call anyway?' she says. 'I'm only away for one night, Joe! Don't tell me the kids miss me, because I'm sure they don't. They won't even know I've gone. This is the first time I've been away on my own since Ollie was born. Do you realise that? The first bloody time! I just want to be here, on my own, at this wedding. I just want to be able to be away from all of you and be a grown-up for once!'

The drunken woman is peeing loudly in a cubicle down the far end, but Meg is dimly aware that, even over the sound of that, this stranger will be able to hear every word of what she's saying to Joe. She suddenly, desperately wants to be sober. She wants to rewind this conversation, right back to the beginning, and say hello properly to the husband she loves more than anyone else on the planet.

'Listen, we'll leave you to it,' Joe's saying. 'It's getting late anyway.'

'I just want to be a grown-up,' Meg whispers, too softly for him to hear.

There is more clattering on the other end of the phone and then a roar of anger from Tallulah. 'Daddeeeeeee!' Meg imagines her stuck in her booster seat, bored and trying to get her father's attention, throwing her plate and bits of leftover food across the kitchen table and onto the floor beside her.

'Oh, bloody hell, Lula!' Joe's voice isn't apologetic anymore. 'Now look what you've done. Listen, Meg, I shouldn't have called – you're clearly not in the right mood for this. I'm sure you're having a great time there, with all your wonderful mates. Of course you don't want to talk to us.'

'It's not that I don't want to talk to you, it's just...'

A wailing has started up and Meg can hear Tallulah's pudgy little hands banging on the table.

'Joe,' Meg says. 'I'm sorry.' But it comes out too softly and the wailing is gathering pace. Tallulah is tired and frustrated; Meg recognises the sound so well. Bedtime will be hard work.

'Right,' Joe is saying. 'I've got to go.' His voice is hard now, clipped. It has lost the softness that was there at the start, and that's all her fault.

'Please don't go,' she whispers.

'It sounds like the wedding has been amazing and you're having a great time. Send my love to Polly.'

Then there's an emptiness on the other end of the phone and, when Meg looks at the screen, it has gone dark. She hates herself.

CHAPTER THIRTEEN

As Meg moves onto all fours and starts to push herself back up to standing, the woman emerges from the loo at the far end, staggering across to the basins and making a noisy attempt to wash her hands, flicking them under the tap so energetically that water splashes down the front of her dress and onto the tiled floor. Meg wants to say something, to explain the phone conversation she's just had and justify herself to this stranger.

But, as she watches, she realises there's no point. She herself is drunk, but this woman is far worse. She sways as she stands by the basin, her head dipping towards the mirror and away again as she screws up her eyes and tries to focus on her own face; when she turns towards the hand-dryer on the far wall, her hip cannons into it. 'Oops!' she shrieks, turning round and giggling at Meg. 'Bit sloshed. That's gonna hurt like fuck tomorrow!'

Meg smiles and steps to one side as the woman staggers past her to the exit, pulling open the door with such force that it crashes against the wall before ricocheting shut again. Meg waits for a few seconds, then unsteadily follows her into the hotel reception. There are so many people out here that she almost has to push her way through. She needs some air, so heads for the front door and goes gingerly down the steps – holding tightly to the handrail – before weaving off to one side and finding a bench.

Now that the sun has gone down, it's freezing out here. A breeze has picked up and it whips the edge of Meg's flimsy dress. She shivers and rubs her hands up and down on her arms to warm them up. Why on earth did Polly decide to have her wedding at the start of January? Surely it would have made more sense to wait until the summer – or the spring at least. Meg got married in July – which had felt like a perfect time to do it, until she and Joe started looking for venues and caterers and realised you needed to book those sorts of things ridiculously far in advance to get anyone decent without paying through the nose. Although, it doesn't feel as if money was a consideration with this wedding: no expense has been spared on anything from the venue and the bride's outfit, to the Veuve Clicquot champagne.

Meg rubs her arms harder to get rid of the goosebumps. For a moment, she can't work out what she has done with her cream cardigan, then realises she must have left it on the floor of the ladies. She ought to go back in and find it, but can't be bothered. An ache in her bladder is reminding her what she'd been on her way to do in the first place, when her mobile started to ring.

The trauma of the call with Joe took her mind off her need to wee but, as the urge rushes back, she crosses her legs and wriggles her bottom further onto the bench: however cold and desperate she is, she isn't going to let herself go inside the hotel again until she has sobered up. So much for the coffee that was being served in the marquee – it doesn't seem to have done her any good. Although, now she comes to think about it, she can't actually remember drinking any of whatever was poured into the cup and saucer that was placed in front of her.

A young couple are sitting on a low wall nearby, a bottle of wine propped up to one side of them, their shoulders pressing into each other. She envies them their closeness. Maybe they got married themselves a few years ago, at a similarly grand hotel in the middle of nowhere? Maybe, like Meg, they have small children and have now escaped from them for the weekend, to come away and celebrate with Adam and Polly. This trip to Wales is special, because it's giving them a chance to spend some quality time together without any guilt or distractions.

'It's just...' the man is saying. 'It's just that... you are one of the most beautiful women I've ever seen. Ever. I don't just mean today. I mean ever – in my entire life.'

The woman snorts with laughter and drops her face into her hands. 'Stop it! You're mad! I bet you say that to everyone you meet. You're such a flirt.'

Definitely not married then, thinks Meg. *At least, not to each other.*

She turns her phone over and presses to light up the screen, hoping she might see a text from Joe, but knowing nothing will be there. Although she's bloated from the rich meal and the numerous glasses of champagne and wine she has knocked back, she also feels strangely empty. It's as if someone has carved out a hole in the pit of her stomach. This is what hurt feels like: hurt, alongside shame, embarrassment, sadness and an overwhelming regret for the way she flew off the handle and snapped at her lovely, kind, caring husband, who encouraged her to come away this weekend and is doing his best to hold things together in her absence – and who had only called her to say hello.

There's no point phoning back now to apologise: both children will be overtired and stroppy at the end of a busy week – Tallulah definitely is, Meg heard that, and goodness knows what kind of a mood Ollie will be in. Whatever happens, bath and bedtime aren't going to be a quick fix for Joe. She'll phone him later, once the children are asleep and he's back downstairs, sitting in front of the TV with a beer in his hand. She will apologise for being such a cow; for biting his head off and making him feel bad for wanting to find out how she was. For caring.

She swipes to open the clock app and saves 8pm as an alarm to remind herself to make the call – with any luck, the kids will have been asleep for ages by then. She isn't likely to forget, but she's pleased with herself for having thought of this, just in case she gets chatting to someone and loses track of the time.

At the thought of Ollie and Tallulah, her pulse quickens slightly. She goes onto her photos and flicks through the pictures she has taken over the last couple of weeks: Tallulah feeding a duck at the park, Ollie proudly showing off his new trainers, Tallulah with eyes closed, screaming with laughter on Joe's lap as he tickles her, Ollie at his friend Barney's birthday party. She breathes in sharply as she comes to those particular pictures.

There are loads of them: the party was held at a local community hall and Barney's mother Julia invited the entire class – which seemed like the only thing you could do when children were in Reception and still forming their friendships, in for a penny and all that. But having sent out the invitations, Julia had confided to Meg that she was relieved every time she received a 'sorry we can't make it' response. 'It's going to be chaos,' she said, as they stood outside the school gates, a few days before the party. 'I've booked a magician to keep them quiet for half an hour, but I'm not sure they'll even sit still for that. Dave thinks we ought to order a bouncy castle too, and put it up in the car park. Do you think that's a bit over the top for a bunch of five-year-olds?'

'Well, possibly,' Meg said. But she really had no idea – she's as new to all this stuff as Julia, and they have both been relying on parents with older children to lead the way when it comes to everything from playdates to birthday parties.

Now, she thinks back to that day as she scrolls through dozens of photos, many of them duplicates. Meg has always taken several photos at a time, intending to go back later and delete most of them, keeping only the best. But invariably she doesn't get round to doing that, so the last time she checked, there were more than 30,000 photos on her phone, the majority of which were taken in the last few years and show her children in various places and poses. Each photo different, yet many also virtually the same.

The birthday party was one of those noisy, hectic afternoons where every parent seemed to have a mobile phone attached to one hand. Most of the pictures Meg took were of Ollie: wearing a paper crown, ripping wrapping paper from a pass-the-parcel, eating at a long table alongside dozens of his classmates, their cheeks smeared with chocolate, their top lips sticky with orange squash.

She flicks through them now, reliving that afternoon as she swipes. At the start of the party, there's Barney opening his presents and the kids playing party games; then there are photos of the magician – a funny little man wearing a top hat and braces – doing his best to entertain an unruly, over-excited bunch of kids. After that, more games. Then the birthday tea and finally a cake being brought out for Barney, sporting five huge fountain candles, which fizzed and sparkled like miniature fireworks.

As her finger scrolls through, Meg realises her pulse is starting to race. There are no photos of what happened towards the end, thank God. But she doesn't need photos: her mind is already replaying it – the crying, her own heartrate galloping, the shocked expressions on the faces of the other parents when she dragged the two boys back into the main hall.

'There you are!' Ali flings herself down onto the bench beside Meg, leaning back and resting her hands on her belly. 'Weren't those speeches *amazing*? I'm so glad Polly spoke as well – she said she was going to, but I got the impression Adam's mother was trying to stop it. She kept saying it wasn't traditional or some such crap. Silly old bat. That woman has a face like a slapped arse – how did she manage to produce such a charming son?' Ali is talking more slowly than usual, her words slurred. 'Hah! God, I am *so* stuffed, I can hardly walk. Look at the state of me, I'm like a bloody hippo.'

Meg glances sideways at Ali's hands resting on her stomach. Her friend's dress is flat across her taut belly, the material not even slightly wrinkled or stretched.

She sighs. 'Yes, Ali, you're gross. Did you actually eat *anything* earlier?'

Even ten years ago, Meg had never been as slim as Ali, but she'd never been overweight either. She'd been a standard size 12 since she hit her teens and she never had to worry about what she ate or whether it would have an impact on the size of her hips.

Looking back, it was extraordinary she was so well adjusted and hang-up free, considering she was the only child of a mother who had been obsessed with weight and on a perpetual diet ever since Meg could remember: Atkins, WeightWatchers, keto, the cabbage soup diet – her mother had tried them all and many others, several times, but remained a stone heavier than she wanted to be.

She also took part in vicarious slimming – telling Meg's father he could do with losing his pot belly and serving him up a steady stream of bland, unappetising meals from whichever faddy diet cookbook was her current favourite. Meg knew he kept a stash of KitKats in his toolbox in the garage and once, after a couple of beers, he admitted to her that he frequently popped into the drive-through McDonalds on the way back from work – a secret she never dreamt of sharing with her mother.

But none of the moaning or banging on about calories ever bothered Meg, and she and her school friends used to work their way through entire packets of chocolate Hobnobs as they laughed at the articles in the *Slimming World* magazines, stacked up beside the sofa.

Then she gave birth to Ollie and found herself carrying extra weight that proved hard to lose. 'It will drop off when you're breastfeeding,' people told her. It didn't. 'You'll slim down when you're running around after him,' the same people insisted. She didn't. Meanwhile, for the first time, her mother's obsession began to make sense and Meg too began to think in terms of good and bad carbs, and type searches like *miracle weight loss programmes* into Google.

Some days it honestly didn't matter. She reminded herself how lucky she was to have two healthy children and a husband who adored her, irrespective of what the bathroom scales told her. But other days, the possibility that she would struggle to get back to being the relatively slim person she'd been at Leeds, brought her down. As did the realisation that she was becoming as hung up about her body as her mother, whose weight obsession she had always mocked. Today had been one of those 'other days' from the moment she got into Ali's Audi outside Hammersmith tube, as she tried not to compare herself to her slim friends or to envy the way their clothes hung so perfectly off their bodies.

The couple sitting on the wall nearby are now leaning backwards and staring up into the sky and giggling.

'What are they doing?' Ali stage-whispers.

'God knows.' Meg is bad tempered all of a sudden; it's the combination of an excess of food and alcohol and an incoming hangover. Plus, she's dog-tired. It has been years since she partied this hard. She and Joe went to a wedding last summer – a friend of his from school – but, after prolonged negotiations, his mother had only agreed to look after the children, on the condition that they were back by bedtime. They had snuck away from the wedding reception before the cake had even been cut and, although they didn't discuss it, Meg knew they both felt short-changed.

'I'm shattered.' Ali stifles a yawn. 'I think the drive from this morning is catching up with me, and drinking in the afternoon is never a good idea – hate to admit Nancy was right – I shouldn't have had all that drink. All that lovely champagne. It was *really* lovely, though I'm feeling a bit shit now. Where is she, by the way? Where's Nancy? Haven't seen her for a while. God, isn't that incredible about her being pregnant? Who'd have thought it. It's nice sitting out here with you, Meg, but I could do with a lie down.'

'Me too,' says Meg. 'But I don't think we can just sneak away.'

'Why not? There's nothing happening at the moment. This is the – what do you call it – the lull, the in-between bit before the evening party starts. That's when the rest of them will turn up, the other guests – second tier guests! Not like us, we're the special ones. But those others who didn't make the list for the ceremony itself. We could head off to our rooms for an hour. I'm sure a power nap would sort me out.'

'Go on, then,' Meg says. The prospect of being able to kick off her painful shoes, undo the straining zip on her dress and collapse onto her hotel bed, is a very appealing one. 'But I don't want to be rude, so let's make it look as if we're just heading to the loo or something.'

They get up from the bench and Meg grabs Ali's arm to stop her toppling over, both of them giggling as they make their way back through the hotel reception and head up the sweeping staircase.

'This is me!' Ali sings out as they get to the first floor, and she lurches off down the corridor.

Meg is staying on the top floor and there are no lifts, so she takes off her shoes before she begins to climb the next narrower flight of stairs, no longer caring what anybody thinks. When she finally reaches her room, she is out of breath and her head is thumping.

The room has sloping ceilings and a cramped ensuite built into the eaves. It was servants' quarters in years gone by, when this fancy hotel was a country house. When she booked, she went for the cheapest single they had available – which still set her back more than £100 for the night. She'd felt so guilty as she read out her card details over the phone: Tallulah's nursery fees had just gone up, yet again, and they hadn't cleared the balance on their joint credit card from last month. Everything costs so much nowadays, and £100 is such a lot of money for one night away – especially considering the size of the room.

But right now, she doesn't care that she's staying in a poky little attic – she's so exhausted she would happily collapse onto straw bales in a stable block. She bends over and drinks some water from the cold tap in the bathroom, before staggering across to the bed and falling sideways onto it. The beautifully ironed white sheets are cool beneath her cheek and she can smell something floral and vaguely familiar: possibly the same fabric conditioner she uses at home.

What will Ali's room be like, down below? She and Nancy probably paid more to stay in large, luxurious suites, but so what? Meg doesn't need space, she never has – she's used to sharing everything. The double bed at home always seems small, but that's because there are sometimes four of them in there jostling for position, with her and Joe stuck on the outer edges, tugging at the duvet, trying to avoid falling onto the floor or getting bruised by wriggling limbs. This lovely soft hotel bed, pushed up against one wall beneath a sloping ceiling, may only be a single, but it feels positively vast in comparison.

She closes her eyes and feels the world close in around her as she starts to doze off.

CHAPTER FOURTEEN

A n insistent beeping is hijacking her dream, pulling her away from the surreal places her mind has been taking her in deep sleep. Meg wakes with a jolt, throwing out her left arm to one side, her fingers crashing against the wall. The beeping continues, and she realises it's coming from her phone. She rolls over and reaches towards the bedside table, but the mobile isn't there. By the time she sees it has fallen onto the carpet, she's fully awake, but suddenly so heavy-headed, she feels sick. She presses to light up the phone screen: 8pm.

'Shit,' she mutters. 'Shit, shit.'

What time did Ali say the evening party started? Meg can't remember her saying a time, but it was definitely earlier than this. She shouldn't have slept for so long: she was only intending to shut her eyes for twenty minutes or so. She rolls herself out of the bed, feeling heavy and sluggish, and staggers across to the ensuite, where she splashes water on her face, before catching sight of herself in the mirror above the basin. Her mascara has smudged under one eye and her hair looks awful. She licks her finger and rubs at the black mark on her skin, which shows no sign of moving. God, did she even bring any make-up remover with her? If not, she'll have to use soap; she can't go downstairs looking like this.

As she walks back into the bedroom, her stomach is churning and she's slightly dizzy. She sits on the edge of the bed and takes some deep breaths, in and out. This is the beginning of a hangover: that's the trouble with starting drinking so early in the day. But she needs to pull herself together and make it downstairs. There's a band playing this evening, then a disco later. And didn't Polly say something about pulled pork rolls? Meg is extremely partial to pulled pork.

'Come on,' she tells herself. 'Back at it.'

There's a glass on the bedside table, half full of white wine; she must have brought it up with her earlier. In a situation like this, the best thing is to keep drinking. She picks it up and takes a long gulp, feeling the liquid slide down her throat. She can hear shouting coming from outside on the lawn at the back of the hotel, and there's music playing somewhere now. It's something classical and very intense; it sounds as if they've set up an entire orchestra downstairs.

As she scrubs the make-up from under her eyes and reapplies mascara, Meg knocks back the rest of the wine. She must ask Polly or Adam where they bought this – the label on the bottle at the lunch table said it was a chenin blanc and it's way more delicious than the cheap pinot grigio she and Joe buy at Aldi. No wonder it's slipping down so easily.

Right, she can do this. She sits down on the bed and tries to slide her feet back into the shoes, but her right heel is a bloody mess with bits of skin hanging off. She winces as she pulls away what remains of the original plaster and hunts around in her bag for another one, then adds a second plaster onto the other heel – just in case. She stands up and breathes in as she hoicks up the zip at the back of her dress. It catches briefly and she has another go. 'Steady,' she mutters to herself. 'Ruin this and you're buggered. There is no back-up dress.' She snorts with laughter as the zip finally closes and sucks in her stomach as she looks at herself in the mirror on the back of the bedroom door. She really does love this special charity shop dress: it's definitely on the tight side, but even after a full afternoon of eating and drinking, she doesn't look as awful as she was expecting. She'll do.

On the way downstairs, she sees a woman come out of a room on the floor below, and a man emerges from another, further along the corridor. 'Guess we all had the same idea!' says Meg, as they meet at the top of the main staircase. 'Sleeping off some of the booze.'

'It hasn't helped,' says the woman. 'Not sure how I'm going to keep going for several more hours!'

At the bottom of the stairs, a string quartet has appeared – four beautiful young women dressed in matching scarlet ballgowns, who are playing the music Meg heard all the way up in her attic bedroom. She stops to listen. The lead violinist is leaning over her instrument, her hair falling across her shoulder like a golden curtain as her arm flies backwards and forwards across the strings. Meg finds herself swaying in time to the music as she watches; she has never been a fan of classical, but only because she doesn't know much about it. Whatever is being played here is beautiful, so overwhelming in its intensity, it almost takes her breath away.

The quartet comes to the end of the piece and the surrounding crowd of guests applaud enthusiastically. Meg wanders back into the marquee. Some of the large round tables have been cleared away and a dance floor has magically appeared at the far end. Behind it, a band is setting up: two men and a woman are adjusting microphones and amps, tuning guitars. A third, rather large man is squashed behind an extremely small drumkit, which looks like it belongs to a child. Meg wonders if he has been wedged into place for the duration of the evening and will need to be pulled out again later by his fellow musicians. She giggles at the image in her head. Maybe this man and the drumkit don't actually come apart? He and it might need to be loaded onto a trolley together later and wheeled home again.

Suddenly there's something dragging at her arm. Turning, she sees a hand belonging to Jade – or Janey, or whatever she's called.

'*There* you are!' Jade or Janey has a glass of champagne in her other hand, which she is slopping onto the carpet. 'I was wondering what happened to you.'

'Hello!' says Meg. 'I haven't seen you in *ages*.'

'Well, I've been right here,' says Jade/Janey. 'Or not *right* here, obviously. I've been all over the place in fact. Hasn't this been a great day? Shall we go and get a little drink?'

It suddenly seems very important to Meg that she owns up and tells this girl that she doesn't have a clue what her name is. It's not fair to pretend to know her, and there doesn't seem to be any other way round it. Sooner or later, she's going to have to fess up. 'Listen,' she says, solemnly. 'I've got something very important to say to you.'

Jade/Janey nods and dips her head to one side, squinting in an attempt to look attentive.

'The thing is,' Meg continues. 'I don't want this to sound rude or anything, but I have no idea who you are or how we know each other!'

Jade/Janey claps her hand across her mouth and they stand staring at each other for a few seconds, before her shoulders begin to shake; for a second Meg thinks she's crying, and is appalled at herself. How could she have been so unkind? She should have just carried on pretending to know this girl and then later on, somehow, she could have tried to wheedle her name out of her.

Then she realises Jade/Janey is laughing. She's laughing so hard she is doubling over and clutching at her stomach. It's infectious and Meg finds herself joining in. Suddenly the two of them are leaning against each other, cackling.

'It's Susie!' the woman says, between snorts of laughter.

'What's Susie?' Meg asks, catching her breath.

'My name is Susie! I have no idea how we know each other either. In fact, I don't think we do. But you looked so friendly outside the church, and I don't know anyone else at this wedding, so I thought we could hang out.'

That sets them off again and Meg's stomach is aching as she clutches at it, her free arm around the other woman's shoulders. 'Do you even know *my* name?' she asks eventually, as the laughter dies down and they step apart again, breathing heavily and grinning at each other.

'Nope, not a clue.'

'I'm Meg. Pleased to meet you.'

'You too.'

Meg can't stop smiling. She likes this new friend very much. 'I'm sorry you don't know anyone,' she says. 'But why are you even here?'

'I know Adam from school,' Susie says, wiping tears from her eyes. 'Our mate Rob was meant to be coming too but he's got Covid.'

This sets them off again and they screech with laughter.

'Poor Rob,' snorts Meg.

'Yes, poor Rob,' Susie agrees. 'But I've got you instead now. Shall we go and do some vodka shots in the bar?'

'Excellent idea.'

Meg lets Susie take her hand and drag her back out of the marquee. As they go past the string quartet, she catches the eye of the girl on the violin and gives her a little wave. 'I love your violining!' she says. 'You're very good! Keep at it!'

'Two vodka shots, please!' Susie yells, as they reach the bar. 'For me and my very nice new friend.'

She turns and grins at Meg, who grins back. She has had several extremely dodgy experiences with vodka in the past; this is a really bad idea.

CHAPTER FIFTEEN

'Meg, what the hell are you doing?' Nancy appears shortly after Meg has knocked back her second vodka.

'Bloody hell,' wheezes Meg. 'That's good.' As the fiery liquid rushes down her gullet and explodes in her pit of her belly, she squeezes her eyes shut. She isn't sure if it really is good, but it has definitely gone down more smoothly than the first, which made her choke so badly that for a few seconds she couldn't open her eyes and it felt as if most of the vodka was going to spurt back out of her nose.

'Nancy!' she continues, her throat still constricted and her voice raspy. 'This is my very good friend, Susie. She wasn't my friend when we got here, in fact I didn't know her at all. But she's really lovely and her name isn't Jane or anything like that. Susie, this is Nancy, who is someone I have known for years and years and who can be quite scary until you get to know her. Actually, she is still scary when you know her better, but she might not be as judgy and hard-nosed with you as she is with me.'

Susie puts out her hand and leans so far forward that she starts to topple over. 'Delighted to meet you.'

Nancy ignores Susie's outstretched hand and is looking at the pair of them as if they've grown antlers from which they have hung several pairs of their own knickers. 'Jesus Christ,' she says. 'How much have you had to drink, Meg?'

'Not enough,' says Meg.

'Not nearly enough,' agrees Susie.

'Do you think you ought to slow down?'

Meg puts her head on one side, trying to look pensive, her forefinger resting up against her chin. 'Do I think I ought to slow down? Hmmm. You know what? I don't think I ought to do that, Nancy. I think I'm having a very good time and I'm going to have another vodka.'

Beside her, Susie cheers and topples sideways onto the bar, where she starts waving frantically to attract the attention of one of the barmen.

'Meg, I have never seen you so drunk,' Nancy says. 'You're going to feel like shit in the morning.'

'Oh blah, blah, blah, sorry Captain Sensible.' Meg glares at Nancy. 'Just for once in my life, I'm having a good time.' To emphasise what she's saying, she digs her finger into Nancy's chest as she enunciates each word. 'Just. For. Once. Because – as you've told me yourself, so many times – my life is dull and boring, and I'm dull and boring, so I've decided it's about time to stop being dull and boring.'

Nancy is shaking her head. 'Meg, I've never told you that, don't be ridiculous. I know you're pissed, but that's unfair.'

'Oh, poor Nancy! Am I being unfair? Did I hurt your feelings?'

'Okay, there is no point in having this conversation with you, right now.' Nancy begins to turn away.

'That's right, just walk off!' Meg calls after her. She doesn't think she said it overly loudly, but everyone around her turns to stare. She tries to smile at Nancy and beckons her back with her forefinger. 'Okay, sorry. Was I shouting? But seriously, don't just walk away, Nancy! I'm having a good time – I'm letting my hair down a bit and having a few drinks with my friend here, whose name is Susie, by the way.'

'I know what her name is.' Nancy crosses her arms and glares at Meg.

'Oh, do you know her as well?'

'No, Meg. You just told me her name, about twenty seconds ago.'

Meg throws out her hand to steady herself, grabbing Nancy's arm. 'Sorry to be boring! Didn't realise I was repeating myself. So sorry. Silly me.' A hiccup suddenly builds up in her throat and it's out before she can do anything to stop it. She shoves her hand in front of her mouth and starts giggling. 'Oops. Sorry again. But seriously, Nancy, you need to lighten up a bit. Do you want one of these vodka things that we're doing, me and Susie?'

'No, I really don't.'

'*No, I really don't,*' Meg mimics. 'God, Nancy, you're telling *me* off for it, but when did you get to be so *boring*! You used to be much more fun than this, years ago. How does Jeff put up with you being so sensible?'

Even in her pissed state, Meg notices Nancy's expression tighten.

'Oh, but there isn't a Jeff anymore, is there?' she carries on. 'Oops, sorry! But just lighten up a bit! I know you're doing an oh-so-grown-up and important job, and I know your life is *so* much more interesting and fulfilling than mine. But that doesn't mean you can't let your hair down. Did you act like a teacher with Jeff, and tell him off like this when you were going out with him, if he had a couple of beers and came home wrecked? Did you make him stand in the corner if he didn't clear up the mess he left in the kitchen? Did you put him in detention if he got back late from work?'

Meg thinks she's being incredibly witty. She sniggers and tries to stand up straight, staggering back and nearly falling over in her stilettos.

'I'm not going to react to any of this, because you're so pissed you won't even remember you said any of it by tomorrow,' Nancy says.

'I absolutely will remember all of it!'

Nancy is shaking her head, her arms still crossed. 'Maybe just slow down a bit, Meg, okay? You are going to feel awful in the morning and we don't want to have to stop the car all the way back up the M4 because you need to throw up on the hard shoulder.'

'Ah, so that's it!' Meg sticks her hands on her waist and puffs out her chest. 'It's not a concern for me, and my physical... my physicalness. My wellbeing, that's what I'm talking about. You're just worried about getting home. The journey back... the journey back to... back to, wherever we're going.'

Nancy starts to turn away, but Meg grabs her arm. 'It's just as well you dumped Jeff, isn't it. It's just as well he isn't here, because you were getting super friendly with Toby earlier. You're right, he's very gorgeous. But you were *all* over him. Does he know you're... shh! You know, that you're...?' Meg mimes a pregnant belly with her hand.

Nancy leans in towards her, eyes blazing. 'Fuck off,' she says.

'Here, we go.' Susie is at her side again, holding two more shot glasses. 'This one is raspberry.'

'I thought we were drinking vodka?'

'We are, dummy. It's raspberry vodka.'

Meg nods sagely and studies the pink liquid in the glass in front of her. 'Fair enough.' She looks round for Nancy, but she has walked away, and Meg finds she has lost her train of thought anyway.

Somewhere there's a phone ringing. It sounds like her ring tone and it also sounds very near, but Meg can't think about that right now, because she has to knock back the raspberry vodka in her hand before she does anything else. This one is much less fiery than the others – in fact, it tastes a bit like Ribena. She sticks her tongue inside the glass and runs it around to finish off any final traces. Quite nice. She might ask for another one of these.

Susie has upended her empty shot glass and is holding it over her open mouth, waiting for a few last drips. 'Excellent,' she announces as she slams the glass back down on the bar. 'Most bloody excellent. I like you, Meg. You are my kind of person.'

'And mine,' Meg nods. 'You are a person too.'

That phone is still ringing. It might be hers, but does she even have it with her anymore? She pats the outside of her bag and can feel something solid. That's good; she can't remember putting her phone in there, but at least she hasn't lost it. In the back of her mind, there's something niggling at her, something she ought to have done. She has no idea what it is and the harder she tries to chase the thought, the further away it skitters.

She closes her eyes for a second and wills herself to concentrate, but her brain is too fuzzy to settle on anything. It can't be important. She will do it in the morning, whatever it is. Anyway, the ringing has stopped, so it can't have been her phone after all.

CHAPTER SIXTEEN

M eg hasn't seen Polly and Adam for ages. Maybe they've gone to get changed? Someone was talking about their honeymoon being in the Caribbean, or was it Florida? Actually, that might have been a different conversation. It's all such a muddle.

She wanders out of the bar and goes towards the front door of the hotel, leaning against the doorframe, rubbing her bare arms and breathing in the bracing night air. She hopes they haven't left early to go somewhere else for their first night of wedded bliss.

It's such a shame that on their own wedding day the bride and groom have to leave their celebrations before everyone else. That had happened with her and Joe: they'd been booked into the honeymoon suite of a hotel near the station, and her mother had insisted they needed to make a big dramatic exit from the evening reception at about 10pm, when things were still in full swing. 'But that seems so unfair!' she'd said, during one of the interminable planning sessions she'd had with her mother. 'Why can't we stay on and enjoy the evening?'

Her mother had sighed and shaken her head, as if Meg was

really very stupid. 'It's tradition!' she said, as if she was talking to a three-year-old. 'It's what happens at weddings.'

Later, when they came back from their honeymoon, Meg went out with some friends, keen to discuss the wedding and relive the day. But she felt left out, listening to them talk about the fun they'd had during the final two hours at the reception; it sounded as if everyone had a blast without them. Joe didn't seem to mind, but Meg always felt as if she'd missed the best bit of her own party.

Meg realises an elderly man in a morning suit is standing beside her. He breathes beery fumes into her face as he sways and she smiles at him, wondering if he's related to the bride or groom. She is just about to ask, when she feels his hand creeping across her bottom.

Her eyes widen and her mouth drops open; it must be a mistake. He hasn't meant to put his hand there – maybe he was just intending to put it on her arm and missed? That would still be wrong, but not quite as appalling.

She stares at the old man and opens her mouth, trying to find the words to point out what he's done. But he is leaning towards her, grinning, and she can see spittle glistening on his lower lip; his hand is now grasping her left buttock tightly and she feels him squeeze it. She jerks away from him so violently that her head crashes against the door frame behind her and, as she flings out her hand to steady herself, vodka splashes out of the tiny shot glass she's holding.

'Hey!' she stutters. 'You disgusting old shit!'

But the man has already turned away and is wandering back towards the marquee, tilting to the left as if fighting to stay upright in a hurricane.

Meg is so angry and offended, she's finding it hard to catch her breath; for a few seconds she can hardly believe what just happened. Should she go after him? It's not in her nature to make a scene about anything – she usually goes to any lengths to avoid confrontation – but, fired up by alcohol, she wants to right this wrong and tell that man exactly what she thinks of him. It's not as if she has never been felt up by an old lech before, but in this day and age, surely she should be taking a stand against something like this?

Suddenly Susie appears at her side again and starts dragging her towards the bar. 'There you are! I went for a wee and then you disappeared. Come on, let's get that lovely barman to get us a couple more shots.'

'There was this old man,' she says. 'Out there, by the door.' But Susie isn't listening; they've reached the bar now and she's leaning against it, watching liquid being trickled out into two small glasses. Meg decides she can't be bothered to go and find the old man. She can't even be bothered to tell Susie what has just happened. But she isn't going to forget about it, she'll definitely try to think about this again, when she's sobered up a bit. The barman walks away and she picks up one of the full glasses and raises it to her lips, knowing she shouldn't, knowing she has had more than enough to drink – a skinful, as her dad says. But sod it, this vodka is amazing; who knew there were so many different flavours?

'What's this one?' she croaks at Susie, as the alcohol hits the back of her throat and makes her gasp.

'This what?'

'This vodka.'

'Oh.' Susie frowns and studies her empty shot glass. 'Tamarind something. No idea what that means.'

As Meg puts the empty glass onto the bar, an arm snakes around her neck and she lurches backwards. If it's that old fucker again, she's not going to put up with any more of his crap. Eyes blazing, she spins around, but then starts to laugh hysterically with relief when she sees who it is.

'How are you doing, gorgeous Megster?' he asks.

'It's *you!*' she says, far too loudly. 'It's you, lovely Luke. Lovely Luke without the beard.' She runs her free hand across his chin, surprised at how soft his skin feels. 'I'm glad Daniel grew the beard and not you. I'm not very keen on them. On beards I mean. Where have you been?'

'Oh, just here and there,' he says.

His eyes aren't quite focusing on her – or maybe she's the one who can't get him into focus. He's definitely swaying a bit, and they both start laughing as they tip sideways. Meg feels a rush of something for this man, she's not exactly sure what it is: he's very handsome and so wonderfully familiar. Staring up into his slightly unfocused eyes right at this second, takes her straight back to Leeds, back to a time when life was simple and she had more fun, and she could fit into her clothes and wear heels for more than half an hour without risking bleeding to death.

She feels his hands slide down her back. 'You look bloody sexy in that dress,' he says.

Meg is surprised. 'It was £7.50,' she says. 'It was the meant I was dress to wear.' She knows that isn't quite right, but Luke doesn't seem to notice.

'You look curvaceous,' he's saying. 'That's the word, curvaceous. Like J-Lo.'

His hands are now on her backside and, for a second, she worries he's going to feel the outsized shaper pants that are holding everything in beneath the dress. But then he's pulling her towards him, and she closes her eyes as she falls forward. At first her forehead is resting against his soft cheek, and then she moves her head slightly to one side and somehow their lips have connected and he's kissing her and she can't stop herself kissing him back.

Luke's lips are slightly dry and he tastes of wine. It's so long since Meg kissed anyone other than Joe, but she isn't thinking about her husband right now. She's thinking what fun this is, and how strange – but also deliciously thrilling – it is to feel the tip of Luke's tongue work its way slowly between her lips.

And, as she loses herself in this man, she's also thinking about the last time this happened and, despite her drunkenness, she's shocked by how turned on she's feeling. She pushes her body forward against Luke's, running one hand across his shoulders, the other down his lower back.

It was just before the end of their second year. They'd been in his room, with the thud of music from the party downstairs causing the floorboards to vibrate beneath them. There was shouting coming from outside on the street, the sound of singing in the kitchen below. Luke had kicked the door shut behind them, pushing her against it as his hands ran under her T-shirt and unzipped her jeans.

They'd both been drinking, but not so much that they didn't know what they were doing. She'd been turned on then too, so massively turned on that she could hardly breathe. She pulled him towards her, not caring about anything else, and the sex was sudden and hard and almost painful, but it was what she wanted. It had only happened once, although Meg longed for that one night to lead to something more. She tried to be cool about the whole thing, shrugging it off when the others asked her about it, pretending it was just a fling, which suited her fine. She wasn't ready for a relationship right now, she insisted; anyway, Luke was such a flirt – it definitely wasn't serious. All lies and pretence, and very hard to maintain.

She pined for him for months and when she saw him with other girls – which happened fairly often – it was as if she'd been slapped in the face. For a long time afterwards, she wondered if he'd been the one that got away. Even when she started going out with Joe, a few months later, her heart still flipped when she caught sight of Luke in the distance, or heard someone talking about him.

And now, after all these years, it's happening again. She's kissing Luke and losing herself to him. The blood is pumping around her head, her body feels as if it might explode. His hands are wandering across her body just as she'd imagined so many times all those years ago. In some ways, it feels as if nothing has changed in the last nine years. But she knows that's not true – everything has changed. Last time she found herself this close to Luke, it wasn't wrong, because neither of them was involved with anyone else. That's not the case anymore, and she really shouldn't be doing this.

Then, just as suddenly as it began, it's over. Luke pulls away and she opens her eyes in surprise to see him stepping back from her and turning to one side, greeting some bloke Meg doesn't know, who's clapping him on the shoulder and offering to get him a drink. Luke still has one hand on her waist, but his grip isn't so tight anymore. She gasps, suddenly realising she needs to take in deep lungsful of air because she must have been holding her breath.

She still has her hand on his back, but then he's dragged away and she's left swaying, her arm outstretched as if pleading with him to come back to her.

'Oooh, who is *that*?' Susie is suddenly in her face, grinning, pulling on her other arm. 'He's rather bloody gorgeous.'

Meg nods. Tries to find something to say. 'Yes,' she manages, at last. 'He is most bloody gorgeous.'

'So, who is he?'

'Oh, no one special. Just my friend, Luke. Lovely Luke.'

Susie narrows her eyes. 'More than a friend, if you ask me.'

CHAPTER SEVENTEEN

M eg is out-of-control drunk. She knows it, but also knows it's far too late to do anything about it. Someone put a glass of water in her hand earlier – she has no idea who – but she took a couple of sips and put it down again, and now she can't remember where she put it, which is a *bad* thing because water is most definitely what she needs right now. Or coffee. She spins around looking for one of those young waiters, but there are none of them in sight, and definitely no coffee pots.

That band has started playing in the marquee, and they're surprisingly good. She hasn't danced like this in *years,* and it's so much fun. Her dress has started to feel tight, so a little while ago she undid the zip a bit – just at the top, so her arms have more room to move around.

There was some guy watching and laughing at her, so she went up to him and grabbed his hands, made him swing about with her. He seemed to be having a very good time.

Everyone is having a good time. Loads of people nearby are laughing with her, although their faces are going a bit blurry, especially when she spins around. In fact, she really shouldn't spin around, because it makes her feel like throwing up.

But it's brilliant, all this dancing! It's totally, utterly brilliant! Best of all, it's not like her to be doing this. Not like her at all. Or not like the quiet, *sweet* little Meg they all think they know now. But, so fucking what? It's about time she showed them she's just as capable as they are, of having a *bloody* good time. This is how she used to be, before she stepped away from the exciting sort of life she used to lead, and into suburban married bliss. Not that there's anything wrong with suburban married bliss, but it feels so good to behave a bit badly again.

The band start playing familiar chords and she claps her hands above her head. 'I love this song!' she hears herself yell. 'It's my favourite, it's my most favourite ever!' She can't actually remember what the song is, but she knows she likes it.

Suddenly Meg realises she's hobbling on the edge of the dance floor, but can't work out why. She's uneven, thrown off balance. What's happened? Looking down, she realises she's only wearing one shoe. Where the hell is the other one? She didn't feel it come loose, which is strange because her feet were so puffy earlier when she woke up from her sleep, she remembers having to virtually shove them into these bloody shoes.

She laughs: that's actually quite funny because these shoes are literally bloody, because of those blisters – which hurt so much, that they've almost stopped hurting. Isn't that weird? It's matter over mind. Mind over matter. Whatever. It's like childbirth – if you tell yourself you can cope with the pain, it doesn't hurt nearly so much. Apparently. Although, actually that's a load of bollocks. Where is that shoe? It must be around somewhere.

Meg drops to her knees and feels around on the dancefloor with her hands. It's hard to see anything down here – except other people's feet! She starts to giggle; it's actually quite good being down on all fours, she doesn't feel like she's about to topple over any longer. But there are so many feet! Some of them are quite close; a man's polished brogue brushes against her hand and she whips her fingers away quickly before he tramples on them, then slaps at his ankles to warn him to keep out of her way.

Shoe. She is looking for her shoe. She turns around and crawls off the dancefloor towards a table. It must be here somewhere.

'Shoe!' she calls. 'Shoe, where are you?'

But it's very dark under the table, and crawling around on this flooring is quite uncomfortable. Meg's left palm lands on something soft that squelches and she draws her hand back in disgust, not able to see what it is. She tries to bring her hand closer to her face, but she still can't see anything. She must get out from under this table. She starts crawling backwards as fast as she can, which isn't very fast because she's feeling a bit sick now that she's down here and moving backwards isn't easy. She has to shuffle each knee in turn. She's aware that her dress has ridden up at the back, but when she tries to move one hand to pull it down again, she loses her balance and topples over onto her side.

'Oops,' she giggles. 'Oh dear.'

Then someone takes hold of her arm and she feels herself being hoisted upwards to a sitting position.

'Are you alright?' It's a woman's voice: measured, mature.

Meg tries to nod but that makes her feel even more sick, so she just smiles, hoping that will tell this nice well-spoken lady she is absolutely fine.

'Give me your arm. Let's get you up,' the woman is saying.

Meg is struggling to hear her above the noise of the band, which has now started playing another song she really, really loves. She eventually staggers to her feet and finds herself face to face with Polly's mother.

'Oh, it's you!' she says. 'I'm so happy to see you. Do you like this song? I love it.'

The woman is smiling at her, but it's not an unkind smile. 'I think you need some fresh air,' she says. 'Do you want to come outside with me?'

'I don't think so, but thank you for asking. I'm going to dance.'

'Are you sure? I wonder if it might be more sensible to have a sit down somewhere. Come over here.' Polly's mother has taken Meg's arm and is leading her gently towards a nearby table. Meg stares at her, amazed that this woman still looks so beautifully turned out and presentable at the end of such a long, stressful day. She wants to vocalise this, but as quickly as the thought comes into her mind, it flits away again and, although she knows she has something very important to say, she can't remember what it is.

She lets herself be guided to a seat, which is shrouded in darkness at the edge of the marquee, and Polly's mother waits until she slumps into it, then reaches across the table for a glass and fills it with water. 'Have some of this. I'm sure it will make you feel better.'

'Oh, you are so kind!' Meg says. 'You are such a lovely lady. We met, you know, a long time ago. Years. When I was... not sure. But I came to your house. The one you live in. I don't know if you still live in it now, though. You were there and you had...' She has lost her train of thought again. It's very frustrating. She has all these things to say, but for some reason she keeps forgetting what they are. Polly is lucky to have such a kind mother, she must remember to tell her that, when she gets back from her honeymoon.

Meg can't imagine her own mother being this thoughtful; she has never had much time for Meg's contemporaries.

She would be welcoming enough when Meg brought

friends home from school and college, but she wasn't a woman who hugged anyone other than her own family and even that form of affection was reserved for birthdays and Christmas.

When both her parents talked with Meg's friends, they were formal and polite, which meant they came across as stiff – sometimes positively unfriendly.

Throughout her teenage years in particular, Meg longed for her mother to be different. She was jealous when she went to other people's houses and their parents greeted her like a friend, and gave her a hug and kissed her goodbye when she left and told her to come and visit them again, any time. It made her feel special and loved and she desperately wanted to come from a family where that sort of tenderness and affection was on constant display. Even thinking that way made her feel guilty though, because there was nothing wrong with her upbringing; her parents were always loving and supportive, just a little old fashioned.

Right now, if this was her wedding, her mother would be doing that thing with her lips, pushing them together tightly so all the skin crinkles up around them. She'd be tutting as well and rolling her eyes at Meg's dad, who would just shrug his shoulders and have another glass of wine.

But Polly's beautiful mother is wonderful and Meg is sure she's the hugging type. 'Did you do that?' she asks her now. 'With her friends, I mean. At your house?'

Even in the darkness, she registers Polly's mother frowning in confusion. But then she smiles and picks up Meg's hand and wraps it around the glass, before helping Meg lift it to her lips. 'Here we are,' she is saying. 'Have some more of this water. It will make you feel much better.'

Meg starts to laugh: this is hysterical, she is *more* than capable of drinking from the glass, but she doesn't want to offend Polly's lovely, pretty mother, so she will just let her do this funny thing with her hand. She takes a sip and nods, trying to pass on a non-verbal message that she's absolutely fine and that this water is delicious. Actually, it's not. It's tepid, which isn't nice at all. Maybe there was ice in it earlier, but it's so warm in here, what with all the people dancing, that the ice has melted.

The music stops suddenly and people start to clap. Meg wants to join them, because this band has been amazing, but she forgets she has a glass of water in one hand and it tips all over the table when she tries to put her hands together. 'Whoops!' she says, as Polly's mother swoops in and takes the glass from her. 'Big whoops.'

Someone cackles with laughter next to her and she turns to the side to see who it is.

'Fuck!' she says. 'It's you!'

'Let me mop up this water.' Polly's mother is leaning across the table, dabbing at the soaking tablecloth with a napkin.

Meg grabs at her arm. 'Look! It's him!'

Polly's mother looks at her in confusion. 'Sorry?'

'Him!' Meg is yelling now. 'It's that fucking lecherous old bugger.'

Polly's mother is now looking past her at the elderly man. She frowns and shrugs her shoulders, as if to say that she doesn't know what Meg is talking about.

'He put his hand on my arse!' Meg shouts, pointing at the man.

There are people sitting across the table, she sees now, and others standing up nearby. Everyone has turned in her direction and, although she realises her voice is very loud now the band has stopped playing and the guests have stopped clapping, she can't do anything about that. She doesn't want to either; she needs all these people to know what this man did to her earlier, when they were standing out in the main reception area.

'This old guy, this one sitting right here, next to me. He put his filthy, horrible hand on my backside and he was squeezing it! I kid you not. Squeezing!' She is still pointing at the old man, although there is no need to point because he's less than three feet away from her and it must be quite obvious to everyone that she's referring to him.

She turns to look at Polly's mother again. 'Can you believe it? He must be ninety-five if he's a fucking day. Jesus, I mean, what a disgusting way to behave at a wedding.' She turns back to the old man. 'Listen, I know things were done differently in your day, mate, but times have changed and in the modern world you *do not* stick your hand on a woman's arse!' She is feeling very self-righteous now. It's important she lets everyone know what this man has done, because nowadays that kind of behaviour is unacceptable. She turns back to Polly's mother, expecting to see sympathy on her face, possibly shock as well – this is her own daughter's wedding after all.

There is a definite expression on the woman's face, but Meg can't quite work out what it is. There's another man behind her, leaning into the table, putting his hand on Polly's mother's shoulder, saying something in her ear. She straightens up and looks past Meg to where the old man is sitting.

Hah, thinks Meg. *Finally! Now he's for it.* This is good that she pointed him out, because at the very least he'll be made to apologise for what he did to her and hopefully that will mean he won't do the same thing to anyone else.

'Don't worry, Dad, she's very drunk,' Polly's mother is saying. 'Leave this to me.'

Meg isn't sure who she's talking about, but needs to make sure everyone understands what she's trying to say. 'He's a lech!' she says. 'This old man, right here, is a nasty...' Yet again, what she had lined up to say, seems to fly out of her brain and she finds herself scrabbling around for the right words. 'He *is*...' she says. 'That. Just that. He is that.'

A middle-aged woman has put her arm on the old man's shoulder and is helping him get up from the table. They are joined by another man, who glares at Meg, then both start to lead him away.

'Hey!' Meg yells. 'Where are you going?'

'That's quite enough.' Polly's mother isn't sounding friendly or concerned any more. She's sounding angry. 'You've had far too much to drink and you're out of control. I'm guessing you're staying here at the hotel, because you're in no state to drive anywhere, so I'm going to find someone to take you up to your room.'

'But what about...?' Meg is confused. She slumps back in her chair. Strangely, she can't quite remember what she was going to say, or why it matters. And she has no idea what Polly's mother is cross about. One moment she was smiling and looking calm and pretty, but then the next, her face has gone all hard. Meg is so confused. It's a shame because she really likes Polly's mother and they were getting on so well!

CHAPTER EIGHTEEN

'Don't worry, I've got her.'

Someone is grabbing Meg's arm and pulling her up. The suddenness of the movement causes everything around her to spin, her stomach lurching in the process. 'Ow!' she yelps. 'Get off me.' The band has started playing again and everything is very loud, but she doesn't feel like dancing now. Polly's mother seems to have disappeared, but Meg wants to try and find her because she is hoping they can talk some more.

'What are you doing, Meg?'

'Get off, you're hurting.'

'Stop making an idiot of yourself!' Nancy's face is inches away, her forehead creased, her eyes blazing. 'You're totally rat-arsed and you're behaving really badly.'

'Oh, FUCK YOU!' Meg yells.

Even over the throb of the band's bass guitar, this comes out louder than she'd expected. Heads turn nearby and a woman tuts in disgust. 'And you can sod off, as well,' Meg shouts at the woman. 'This is a private... this private is a... it's a conversation.'

She feels herself lurching to one side and realises Nancy is dragging her along the edge of the marquee towards the exit. She is pulling hard and Meg stumbles as they go outside onto the grass, which is lit up by the glow of small solar lights around the edges. It's freezing out here and she shivers as Nancy pulls her towards a bench.

'Right, sit down here,' she orders. 'I'm going to fetch you some water. Don't go anywhere or say anything. Just stay put. Understand?'

Meg wants to laugh, but Nancy is already marching away across the grass. Instead, she salutes her friend's departing back. 'Yessir,' she says. She slumps back on the bench and stretches out her legs. Where did that shoe go?

She squints down at her feet and sees she is still wearing one of the blue stilettos. The blisters must have burst again because her heel is throbbing violently. She has no idea what time it is. Did she ever find her cardigan? She knows she left it somewhere, but can't remember where. It was on the floor somewhere, and she'd been sitting there. But it wasn't the floor of the marquee.

She sighs; it's no good, her brain just isn't working properly. Luckily, although it's freezing out here, she isn't feeling cold – probably because she's been dancing so much. Leaning back, she stares upwards. Above her head, strings of fairy lights are draped between the trees and she watches the sparkling lines swaying gently: it's all very magical. Tallulah would love this.

When Nancy comes back, she's carrying a pint glass, full of clear liquid, and is dragging Ali with her. 'Honestly!' she says, pushing Ali towards the bench so that she slumps down beside Meg. 'The two of you are as bad as each other. Meg, drink this, I'll go and get some water for you, Ali. Don't move, either of you.'

'Vodka!' slurs Meg, happily.

'No, water.'

Meg takes a sip. 'Nasty,' she says. 'Vodka is much nicer.' But she downs her pint of water in one, suddenly realising she's got a raging thirst, and wipes the back of her hand across her mouth before belching loudly. 'Sorry, that's gross. I'm far too pissed.'

Ali nods sagely. 'Me too. Bladdered.'

Meg giggles. 'And Nancy is cross.'

'She is.' Ali nods. 'What was going on in there?'

Meg looks at her in confusion. 'Where?'

'In the marquee. You were screaming at Polly's grandfather and it looked as if Polly's mum was about to kill you.'

'Her grandfather?'

'Yes, that old guy in the morning suit.'

'Oh shit.' It takes a few seconds for Meg to compute what she's hearing, and when she does, she isn't sure how it makes her feel. She had no idea the old man with the wandering hands was related to Polly. She can't quite believe it; how can someone as lovely as her, have a grandfather who feels up her friends? This makes everything much worse, because she has just insulted the bride's close family. But, then again, she's still drunk enough to feel bolshy rather than embarrassed.

'I don't care who he is,' she says. 'He put his hand on my arse earlier.'

'Oh God, seriously?'

'Yes! Isn't that gross? So, when I saw him there, I thought I had a right to say something. But I didn't know who he was. Not that it makes a difference!' She is feeling more self-righteous by the second. 'I mean, if he's a dirty old man, he's a dirty old man – even if his granddaughter is getting married, right? That was the point... the point I was trying to make to...'

Her foggy brain lets her down again. She is now feeling so sleepy, she can't actually remember what point she was trying to make. Or who she was trying to make it to. Polly's lovely mother had been there – except then she wasn't being so lovely anymore. In a moment of crashing sobriety, Meg suddenly hopes that none of this gets back to Polly. She loves Polly so much, and was so happy to be invited to this wedding. But now it's all going horribly wrong.

'I don't think it's my fault, though,' she says to Ali. 'Is it my fault? Please don't tell her about any of this.'

'None of this is anyone's fault,' Ali says. 'It's just all a fucking mess. I need to go to bed. But I have to sober up a bit first. God, I've had all I can take of this bloody wedding – I can't wait to get out of here in the morning.'

Meg looks at her in surprise. 'Haven't you had a good time?'

Ali grimaces. 'No, I have not had a good time.'

'But, Ali! This is Polly's wedding! Why haven't you enjoyed it? I've had a really good time. Well, mostly. I think.'

'Good for you.'

Meg is confused. 'I don't understand, why aren't you happy for her?'

'It's just another fancy wedding. Another happy bloody couple. Another embarrassingly huge amount of money blown in one day.'

Meg thinks about this. 'I quite like weddings.'

'Well, bully for you. I could happily live the rest of my life without going to another one.'

'But... this is *Polly's* wedding – our Polly?'

Ali laughs, but there's no humour in it. 'Yes – our Polly. That makes it even worse.'

Meg is confused. Her head is thumping and the water sloshing around in her stomach is making her nauseous. She's also exhausted; given half a chance she could fall asleep right here on this bench, despite the freezing cold and the pain from her bleeding feet and the band blasting out ear-splitting nineties covers just a few feet away.

'Aren't you happy for Polly?' she asks.

'Yes, of course I'm bloody happy for Polly. It's all great, Polly looked amazing, Adam is a fabulous human being, the service was lovely, the cake was delicious, the speeches were funny... blah bloody blah and so on and so forth.'

'What's the matter?' Meg asks. 'Why are you being miserable?'

'I'm not, I'm just tired.'

'Oh God, tell me about tired! You don't know the meaning of the word until you've had babies. When Ollie was born, I didn't get more than two hours sleep at a time for seven months. I was so tired I could barely string two words together. I was walking around like a zombie, and then with Tallulah–'

'For fuck's sake, give it a rest, Meg,' Ali snaps. 'We've heard it all before. We know motherhood is the most important job on the planet. We know how hard it is and how sleep-deprived you are, and how you mostly have to function on five-minute power naps and no one else understands how bad it is unless they've given birth themselves, and even then, they didn't have it half as bad as you did.'

Meg's mouth drops open and she stares at her friend. She wants to say something, but can't think what. Instead, she raises her hand and punches Ali hard on the arm.

'Ow! That hurt!'

'Good! I'm glad it hurt.' She isn't really, but she's indignant. 'Why are you saying all those things? That's horrible.'

'I know,' mutters Ali.

'You're being a bitch.'

'I *know*!' Ali turns and shouts at her now, making Meg jump. 'I know I'm being a bitch. That's me through and through. I'm surprised you haven't found that out by now. This is the real me, Meg – I'm insecure and jealous and resentful and I'm a prize cow. And I'm fed up with pretending my life is perfect and everything is wonderful. I'm fed up with being happy, successful, dynamic Alison Benson.'

Meg frowns. She stares at the profile of her friend's face in the darkness, struggling to understand what's going on. 'Ali,' she whispers. 'What's this about?'

There's a long pause. So long, it turns into a silence – despite the thundering noise coming from the marquee – and Meg isn't sure what she should be saying or doing to break this silence. Then she becomes aware of a soft sound, a whimpering, and sees the dark shape of Ali's shoulders shaking. Her friend is crying.

'I hate all this,' Ali says suddenly, her voice choked, and so low Meg can hardly hear. 'I hate that Polly's getting married. I mean, I like Adam, he's a great guy and all that, but I fucking hate him too.'

Meg is so confused. If Ali likes Adam, how can she hate him as well, and why? This makes no sense. She doesn't know Adam very well, but there's nothing about him that seems remotely hateable. 'That's very strange,' she says.

'No, it's not,' sobs Ali.

'It is, because he's a lovely guy! You just said that?'

'I know, Meg. He's a really lovely guy. But that's got absolutely fuck all to do with it. Don't you get it? Don't you get anything? God, you can be dense sometimes. I hate him because he's got Polly.'

Despite the alcohol coursing through her veins, Meg suddenly feels stone cold sober. For a few seconds, she stares at Ali in the darkness, watching her wipe her eyes. She finally gets it. Jesus, Ali's right – how can she have been so stupid? 'Oh God,' she says, putting her hand on her friend's arm. 'I didn't realise. I'm so sorry.'

Ali sniffs and nods.

'I mean, I had no idea. I really had no idea.' Even as she says it, Meg knows that's not entirely true, but her heart is thundering and she is trying to process so many thoughts that she can't keep up.

She frowns into the darkness, forcing her slow drunken brain to focus. Ali has just shared a major secret, but it's something Meg should have guessed – even if she wasn't let in on it at the time. Daniel said something to her at the table earlier, something about Ali. What was it? She shakes her head in frustration, unable to get to grips with any of this. Ali and Polly; it makes no sense. But the thing is, it also makes perfect sense. Now that she's had time to process it, what she's hearing isn't a huge surprise. Is she the only one not to know about this? None of them have talked about it before – but maybe they just didn't talk about it with her?

Yet again, Meg feels as if she has been stuck on the outside of her own life, peering in at everything through a window but never quite able to work out what her friends on the inside are saying or doing.

'Do you know,' Ali gives a small laugh, which isn't meant as a laugh. 'I came here today, half hoping the wedding wouldn't go ahead. I know how crazy that sounds. Of course, it was always going to go ahead – nothing would have stopped it. Short of me standing up in the back of that church and yelling to make them stop! Hah, wouldn't that have set the cat among the bloody pigeons.'

Meg puts her arm around Ali's shoulders, and sees the tears on her friend's cheeks glistening in the glow of the fairy lights above their heads.

'Stupid isn't it,' Ali says. 'To hold out for someone for such a long time – when you know they don't feel the same and there's not a hope in hell of them ever loving you back in the way you love them.'

'It's not stupid,' Meg says. 'Oh Ali, I feel awful. I wish you'd told me.'

'It only happened once,' Ali says. 'Between me and Polly. One night. It was just a bit of fun for her, I understood that from the start. We were all experimenting back then, and most of the time it didn't mean anything. She said so afterwards and I agreed with her. We laughed about it. But I was lying. It was the biggest lie I'd ever told – that night meant everything to me. Polly meant everything to me. She still does...'

Meg's mind is racing, taking itself back eleven years to the first few weeks at university, when she'd got to know Polly and been introduced to her flatmate. What had she thought of Ali, back then? She really can't remember much about those early days, but Ali had always been friendly and fun to be with.

She had welcomed Meg and happily moved over to create room for her, seeming not to resent that Polly was turning their friendship into a three-way thing. Or maybe she resented it hugely, but had been mature enough not to show it. It was equally as likely that Meg – fresh out of school, naïve and a little bit needy – had missed the signs. She hadn't been looking for them, after all, so if there hadn't been any obvious antipathy or awkwardness, she may have been blissfully unaware that Ali really didn't want her around and would rather have kept Polly to herself.

It was also possible that in those early days at Leeds nothing had yet happened between Ali and Polly. That night they spent together may have come much later – in which case, Meg would have had time to grow closer to both of them and would have believed she knew her two friends pretty well, so it was even more extraordinary she'd missed all the signs.

But it didn't really matter when they'd spent that night

together and Meg certainly couldn't ask Ali for details right now. Other things were flooding into her head: Ali's close relationship with that tutor, Maria; the fact that Ali had never had a relationship at university, or expressed any interest in one; the fact that she hadn't had a relationship since – or not one she'd shared with any of them. Why hadn't she felt able to talk about any of this? No one would have judged her.

There was also the long-ago falling out with her family, rumours that Ali's father had kicked her out and told her she was no longer welcome in the family home. Had that been the result of a discovery about her sexuality? If so, then it was a burden she'd had to carry all by herself, which struck Meg now, even in her drunken state, as unbelievably sad. What a lousy friend she'd been to Ali.

'I sat looking at that wedding present for hours this morning,' Ali laughs, sniffing and wiping the tears from her cheeks with the back of her hand. 'I was awake from 4am, just sitting in the kitchen staring at the box, which I'd wrapped up so carefully, last weekend. At one point I got angry and ripped all the paper off. Then I had to pull myself together and wrap it up again.' She laughs properly now. 'God, what an idiot. I can hear how crazy this all sounds. But I hated that fancy bloody coffee machine. It seemed to be so significant – it wasn't just a wedding present for the happy couple, it meant the end of me and Polly, or, rather, the end of the me and Polly I'd always thought might just be possible, one day. I knew it was unrealistic, but I couldn't stop myself imagining a time when things might change.'

Meg can't think of anything to say, but it doesn't seem to matter. She wonders how long Ali has been bottling up all this.

'I honestly didn't realise I'd left the present behind this morning until I was downstairs, in the car driving away from the flat. But I didn't go back to fetch it, even though I could easily have done that. I'm sorry, it was wrong of me. I should have turned around and gone back for it...'

Meg pulls Ali's head down onto her shoulder and wraps her arms around her, hugging her tightly and rocking her like she rocks her babies. None of what her friend is saying is coming as a shock. In fact, the only surprising thing about all of this, is how unsurprised Meg feels.

CHAPTER NINETEEN

'Right, take this!' Nancy appears out of nowhere and is standing in front of them with another pint glass in her hand. 'See what I mean?' she says, turning to speak to someone behind her. 'They're pissed as farts, the pair of them.'

Meg can make out a shape behind Nancy – it's a man, and she thinks it may be Toby, although it's too dark to see his face. Nancy stops talking and leans in closer. 'Al, are you crying?'

Ali pulls herself upright, out of Meg's arms, swiping at her eyes.

'Jeez, you are! What's the matter? What's going on?'

'Nothing,' Ali says. 'Nothing is going on. I'm just pissed and knackered, that's all.'

'Well, it looks like a bit more than that.' Nancy pushes the pint glass out in front of her, towering over them as Ali reaches for it. 'Come on, what the fuck is this all about?'

Ali shakes her head, refusing to look up at her, her hand shaking as she lifts the glass to her lips.

Meg notices the man turn and move away and feels bad she didn't get to say hello again, if it was Toby. She chatted to him briefly across the table at the meal earlier, but Nancy had been draping herself all over him, so his attention hadn't been on anything or anyone else. It's a shame: she always liked Toby. There are so many conversations that aren't getting finished at this wedding.

'Meg! You tell me what's going on,' Nancy persists. 'Why is she crying?'

'Nancy, just leave it, will you.' Ali takes a deep breath and stands up from the bench. 'It's nothing you need bother yourself about. Not that you'd be particularly bothered anyway, but just go back to the party and have a good time.'

'Oh yeah, like I'm about to do that without finding out what little drama you two are involved in!' Nancy says. 'No way! Tell me what's happened?'

Meg wants to defend Ali. This is typical of Nancy, to storm in and insist on being part of it. Nancy hates being left out of anything. For once, Meg feels powerful: Ali has shared a secret with her, and not just any secret – a fucking massive secret that has well and truly messed up the last ten years of her life. But of course, Nancy can't bear to be the one left out, the one who isn't being confided in. Meg needs to join this conversation and defend Ali. She grabs the bench and pushes herself to standing, swaying so far to one side that she almost topples over. 'Nancy!' she announces. But then can't think what else to say.

Nancy reaches out and grabs her arm to steady her, and is now laughing. But it isn't a kind laugh. 'Oh my God, Meg. Look at the state of you! Did you carry on drinking after I saw you in the bar earlier? I did suggest it wasn't a good idea.'

Meg is angry with herself for being so drunk, but even more angry with Nancy. Suddenly the words flow again.

'Just for once, stop being so *right* about everything,' she says. 'You always have to know best, Nancy. You always have to be the one telling us all what to do. And what to say. What to... everything.' Her head is spinning again now. She thought she was sobering up rapidly while Ali was crying a couple of minutes ago, but it turns out she is still wildly and nauseatingly drunk. She feels something catch in her gullet and suddenly realises she's going to throw up.

It happens swiftly and violently. Luckily, she makes it to the shrubbery behind the bench and crouches over as what seems like litres of champagne, wine and vodka erupt out of her body. Her retching is horrifically loud, but the band is hammering out *Dancing Queen* inside the marquee so, even as she worries about the noise she's making, she realises no one else will hear. Apart from Ali and Nancy.

Finally, it's over, and Meg stands back up, wiping her mouth with the back of her hand, breathless and exhausted by the effort of emptying herself of so much alcohol.

Ali has come over while she was throwing up and grabbed a handful of Meg's hair, holding it out of the way. 'You okay?' she asks, rubbing her back.

Meg nods. She is so far from okay that she wants to cry, but she concentrates on standing upright, taking deep breaths in and out.

'Can't say I'm surprised,' Nancy says. 'I've never seen you drink so much. This isn't like you at all, Meg.'

Suddenly, it's all too much for Meg to bear. While she was leaning over in the bushes, throwing up so violently that it felt as if her insides were being ripped from her body, the humiliation was building up inside her along with the bile. But even though she knows she has made a fool of herself and hates being so out of control, the very small part of her brain that is still almost able to function was reassured by the fact that she's with two of her closest friends; at least they will look after her and be sympathetic.

But clearly that isn't the case. Nancy, as always, is putting her down, treating her like an idiot. Nancy is being dismissive and arrogant. Right at this moment, Meg hates Nancy more than she has ever hated anyone in her life. But actually, she has the upper hand, because Ali confided in her: she's the one Ali trusted enough to share her feelings with. She, Meg, is the one who has the power in this situation and she has had enough of being treated like the weakest link in this group.

'You have no idea what is or isn't like me,' she says, stepping forward and squaring up to Nancy. 'You don't know me, Nancy. You think you do; you think I'm just pathetic little Meg, who ruined her life by having babies and giving up her career. But there is *so* much more to me than that.'

She can hear herself still slurring her words and wishes – for the umpteenth time – that she hadn't had so much to drink tonight. 'You think I'm just a frumpy mum. You think my life is boring. You think I've got no backbone!'

Nancy is shaking her head from side to side. 'You're putting all this on yourself, Meg. I don't know where you get this idea that I look down on what you do or the fact that you've had kids. I've never said that.'

'You don't need to say it! You show it in the way you react to everything I talk about. But you're wrong about me. There is so much more to me than you know. And some people value my friendship. Some people like me for who I am!'

Nancy is turning away. 'Whatever, Meg. Go to bed and sober up.'

Meg reaches out and grabs her by the arm, fury welling up inside her. 'Fuck you, Nancy! Why do you always treat me like this? Ali trusts me with things, and tells me secrets, don't you, Al?'

'Shut up, Meg.' Ali's voice is low and brittle.

'No, it's okay,' Meg says. 'Don't worry, I won't tell anyone about you and Polly and what went on. But Nancy just has to stop being such a cow.'

'About her and Polly?' Nancy says.

'Meg, stop talking!' Ali is right behind her now, then Nancy slaps Meg's hand away so hard that it stings.

'Let's stop all this, right now,' Ali is saying. 'We've had too much to drink. We all need to calm down and go to bed.'

But Meg is feeling reckless and out of control. She doesn't want this to be over. She turns to Ali. 'She's such an arrogant bitch,' she says. 'Nancy. Our so-called friend. She thinks she's so much better than us, she thinks she can get...' Turning again, she realises Nancy is walking away from them. 'Come back here!' she yells, but the music is too loud and Nancy doesn't hear her. Or maybe she's ignoring her. Meg starts walking after her, but she can't seem to get her balance and when she looks down, she sees she's still only wearing one stiletto. She swears under her breath and leans down to take the shoe off, nearly collapsing onto the grass in the process. 'Stupid thing,' she mutters. The shoe is so tight around her foot that she has to use both hands to lever it off and it hurts like hell when she does. Grabbing it, she stands up again. There's something wet all over her hands, but it's too dark to see what it is. 'Nancy!' she screams, setting off towards the marquee.

She comes in through an entrance that leads directly onto the dancefloor. It's loud and heaving, there are people everywhere, dancing, twisting, twirling, singing. The band is playing something familiar, but Meg can't think clearly enough to work out what it is. She can see Nancy just ahead of her and pushes past the people nearest the edge of the dancefloor.

Then suddenly, here's Polly! 'Oh my God,' Meg screams. 'I haven't seen you all evening! Where have you been?'

Polly has changed out of her wedding dress and is wearing a pale pink shift that ends just above her knees. Her hair is down now, curling across her shoulders in soft blonde waves. She has her arms raised above her head as she dances, lip synching to the words of the song.

Adam is beside his new wife, dancing as well, but not looking at her now. Instead, he's looking sideways at Nancy, who's trying to push her way past but getting jostled and held back by the crowd.

Meg can't see the expression on Nancy's face, but she can see Adam's. For a moment, she doesn't understand: he's looking concerned. No, not concerned, puzzled. No, that's not right either. Meg can't work it out, but there's something wrong here: there's something that isn't being said. He should be smiling at everyone here tonight, these people are all his friends, guests at his wedding to beautiful Polly. But Adam isn't smiling; Adam is looking like a rabbit caught in the headlights.

Polly is still dancing, but has now seen Meg and is turning towards her, waving and cheering. 'Meg! Hey, are you having fun?'

The realisation is sudden and astounding. Meg stops in the middle of the dancefloor, as someone's flailing arm bashes into her back. Why didn't she see it before? It's so bloody obvious. A girl falls against her, pushing her forward so she stumbles and collides with Polly. The stiletto Meg's holding in one hand knocks against Polly's chest, and with her other hand Meg grabs onto the soft material of her friend's dress to steady herself. But her eyes are still focused on Nancy, a few feet away, who now turns and looks back at her.

Then, the band finishes the song, on one short, sharp note, and Meg exclaims into the sudden silence. 'Oh fuck. It's *his* baby!'

CHAPTER TWENTY

Someone is screaming very loudly in Meg's ear. She cowers and tries to get out of the way, but now hands are pushing her to one side.

'Polly, oh my God!'

'What the hell? Polly are you alright?'

Meg can't work out what's going on, there are too many people talking, moving forward. She looks up. Polly's pale pink dress is covered in slashes of red – along the neckline and further down, near her waist. Polly's arms are raised on either side and she's staring down at herself.

'It's blood!' someone screams. 'She's bleeding!'

An older woman pushes Meg to one side and rushes to Polly, grabbing her arm and holding it up. 'Where's it coming from? Are you hurt, darling? Why are you bleeding? What's happened?' The woman half-turns and Meg sees it's Polly's mother. She shrinks back, knowing this woman won't want to see her, but unable – through a drunken blur – to remember why.

'Someone help?' Polly's mother is calling now.

'No! It's fine!'

'What's going on?' An older man is pushing his way through now.

'It's fine, I'm okay!' Polly's voice is weak beside everyone else's and, at first, they take no notice. She batters away the hands that are trying to take hold of her, then looks up and her eyes meet Meg's. 'Stop, stop, I'm not bleeding. I don't know what this is but it hasn't come from me.'

But then a girl standing beside Meg turns towards her and exclaims in horror, and other people start to stare at her. Meg doesn't know why until she looks down at herself and sees her stiletto, soaked in blood where the skin on her heel has been ripped to shreds. She brings her other hand up to her face and, unbelievably, that's covered in blood as well. There's so much of it, so much blood everywhere. Now that everything has stopped, she realises her foot is throbbing and looking down she sees more blood smeared across it and onto the coir matting below.

'I'm sorry,' she whispers. 'It's me. Oh God I've put blood all over you, Polly. It's from my foot – I'm so sorry, it was an accident.'

But Polly doesn't seem to be listening. She has stopped staring at Meg now and has turned towards Adam. His face is pale; he hasn't moved. When Nancy tried to push past them on the dancefloor, he turned to stare at her; then – after too long – his eyes flickered back to his new wife. They're still locked on her now, but they're too wide, too startled. It's as if his body is waiting for his brain to tell it what to do, how to react.

'What does she mean?' Polly asks him.

There are still people talking all around them, discussing the blood and the ruined dress and exclaiming at the state of Meg's feet. There is hubbub and chaos. A waiter appears with a first aid kit, and Polly's mother starts explaining it has all been a misunderstanding, that the bride is perfectly fine. A woman is dabbing at the front of Polly's dress with a napkin and someone else has taken her arm. All around them, people are talking, calling out, shaking their heads in horror.

But Polly stands stock still at the centre of it all.

'What does she mean?' she asks again, staring at Adam.

Meg suddenly realises Nancy is still here. She wasn't able to fight her way past people and has now been hemmed in as they crowd around the bride and groom, anxious to find out what's going on. She is standing a few feet away, with her arms crossed in front of her and she is staring back at Meg. Someone who didn't know her, might think her face is empty, devoid of expression. Except Meg knows Nancy very well. She knows this blank, neutral expression is masking pure hatred.

'Come on now, everyone!' says Polly's mother in a falsely high cheerful voice. She claps her hands and makes shooing motions. 'Let's give them some space. Everything's fine!'

Nancy is still staring at her, but Meg forces her eyes away. She needs to apologise to Polly, to explain, but she can't think what to say. Her heart is racing so hard she can hardly breathe.

'Adam.' Polly's voice is too quiet to attract much attention; people are still talking all around her. 'What the fuck does she mean about the baby?'

Meg needs to get out of here. She turns around, not sure where the exit is at this end of the marquee, desperate to find a way back into the garden. But there are too many people milling around. Someone must have signalled to the band to carry on playing, because they strike up again, belting out the familiar notes of something from the eighties. It's a song she likes and this time she thinks she almost knows the band – is it Madness? The Specials?

Suddenly, there's a hand on her arm. 'Hey you,' a voice says. 'This way, hold onto me.'

Susie is beside her and Meg lets herself be pulled out through the crowd, elbows knocking into her on all sides.

Dizziness swoops over her in waves, then in a rush they're outside and the freezing fresh air hits her like a slap on the cheeks. She stumbles across to the bench, where she was sitting with Ali just a few minutes ago and collapses onto it.

The bench creaks as Susie sits down next to her and puts an arm around her shoulders. Meg can hear her asking if she's okay, but her voice sounds very far away, almost echoey. She closes her eyes in an attempt to block everything out, but imprinted on her brain are the expressions on the faces of the women she has considered for so many years to be her best friends: Ali furious, Polly confused, Nancy cold and unforgiving.

Everything is spinning around her, and she knows nothing will be the same again.

She has really fucked up this time.

CHAPTER TWENTY-ONE

There's something hard sticking into her cheek. As Meg moves, it knocks against her eye and she twists away too quickly, causing the room to swirl around her. Her head is thumping so badly it feels like a metal skullcap has been screwed into her temples, and her throat is so dry, it's an effort to breathe.

She opens her eyes and sees her phone lying on the pillow beside her. She reaches for it and jabs at the screen several times before realising it's out of charge.

For a couple of seconds, she can't work out where she is, but then it starts to come back to her: Polly's wedding, the sharp outlines of the furniture in her hotel room. She has no idea what the time is, but daylight is streaming through the window. She obviously didn't pull the curtains last night – in fact, it doesn't look like she did anything much last night. She is still wearing her dress and is lying on top of the bedcovers; the door to the ensuite is open and the light is on inside, the extractor fan whirring away, as it has been doing for hours. Looking down, she sees a single blue stiletto, smeared with blood, lying on its side on the carpet.

She moans and closes her eyes again. Everything hurts; she wants to die. She has never felt this horrifically hungover in her life.

From somewhere outside, there's a distant laugh, then a faint clattering, as if plates are being stacked. The prospect of moving from this prone position on the bed is almost more than Meg can contemplate, but she knows she must force herself to sit up and find the charger for her phone. After that, she must get out of this dress and somehow get across the room and into the shower. Then, she must go and find her friends.

Oh shit: her friends. A memory from the evening before hits her with such force, it makes her gasp. She was talking to Ali and Nancy, aware she was slurring, but not caring what they thought. What was that conversation about? How did it start? So much of last night is a blur. Ali was crying, leaning against her, her shoulders shaking.

Then, Nancy was saying something to her, making her feel stupid. Meg knows she yelled at Nancy – for a change, she actually felt like she had the upper hand with her. Then, more images flood into her head: she remembers staggering into the marquee and what she said next.

The shock of it chills her. The words had been inside her head; they were what she was thinking when she saw Nancy trying to get through the crowds and Adam staring after her. But the words should have stayed in her head. She didn't mean for everyone to hear. How can she have done that to Polly? Beautiful, funny, popular Polly, who was supposed to be having the best day of her life.

Meg feels as if she might cry. She wants to be told it was all a dream – a nightmare, rather – that none of it really happened. However drunk she was, however angry she felt with Nancy, what Meg has done is unforgivable.

This is so unlike her! She hates confrontation or doing

anything to upset other people. That's partly why she has been finding the last few months so difficult; not only has she shied away from tackling any of Ollie's bad behaviour, but the awful things that have been happening aren't something she has been able to talk about with her new friends, the fellow parents she has got to know on a superficial level, through toddler group and school.

They would have been shocked and made judgements and there would have been recriminations. That's why she'd been hoping she could discuss some of it with her real friends, this weekend. The friends she has had for years and who knew her when she was just Meg, rather than Ollie's mum.

She tried to start a conversation in the car yesterday, when they were driving to Wales, but neither Nancy nor Ali reacted. Maybe she should have been more up-front and come right out and told them she had a problem and needed some advice. Would they have been interested or cared? Who knows.

A door slams further along the corridor and a couple are talking as they walk past her room towards the stairs. Meg can hear every word. Does this mean everyone in the nearby rooms would have heard her come crashing back up here last night?

She pushes herself up and swings her legs over the side of the bed, waiting until her heaving stomach settles. After half a minute, she takes another deep breath and stands up, reaching behind her for the zip on her dress and realising it's already half undone. Oh, for God's sake, was she walking around all night with her bloody dress nearly falling off? She drags the zip down the rest of the way, wriggles the material over her hips and steps out of it, walking slowly towards the ensuite. She is desperate to pee and, as she sits on the loo, her forehead resting on her hands, she remembers throwing up in the bushes outside last night, then doing it again in here. Please let her have done it quietly, otherwise fellow guests along this corridor would have been lying in bed listening to her retch. The humiliation is so immense, she can hardly bear it.

Back in the bedroom, she plugs her mobile into the charger and waits for what feels like an eternity for it to come back to life. Her dress is lying on the carpet with grass stains down one side; there's no way they'll ever come out. It looks as if she was rolling around on the lawn as well last night. When she picks it up, she sees there's a tear down the other side. She doesn't remember that either and realises she has no idea what happened to her pretty cream cardigan. She can ask at reception, but it will be hugely embarrassing if it has been handed in, covered in vomit.

The phone finally pings into life: it's nearly 9am. Notifications begin to flash up: there's a missed call from Ali, made yesterday evening. At first, she can't work out why Ali would have been calling her, but then realises she must have been trying to find her, probably while Meg was knocking back vodka shots in the bar with Susie. She groans again as she remembers all that – how much vodka did they drink?

Then, there's a text from Joe, sent much earlier this morning:

> Hello Mummy! This is Ollie. We're all okay but we miss you. Hope you're having a good time xxx

It obviously wasn't Ollie who sent it. His spelling isn't that good for a start; anyway, they never let him anywhere near their mobiles, so he doesn't know how to send a text. No, this was Joe, suggesting to their son that they could send her a text and pretend it was from him, because it would be a good way to find out how she was. He was probably wanting to reassure her all was fine at home, but it's likely he might also have been checking up on her. She thinks back to that awful phone conversation after the wedding meal, when she sat on the floor of the ladies and yelled at him for disturbing her on her night away. He got angry too – not surprisingly – and, although she can't remember exactly what was said, she knows the conversation didn't end well. The memory makes her blush with embarrassment.

Did she try to call him back after that? She was going to, she'd been feeling so mean about it and wanted to apologise, but she has an awful feeling she never got round to it. Just as well, she was so pissed she wouldn't have been able to string two words together. But this message from him is clearly a peace offering; she must call him.

Before she does that though, there's someone else she needs to speak to. She scrolls through her contacts, her finger trembling. Jesus, how can she put this right? She presses the name and watches as the screen changes and the phone starts to ring. Are they even still in the country? Maybe they had an early start to get to the airport? Or they may be going nowhere: Meg's stupid uncensored comment last night, might mean there will be no honeymoon.

'Hello?'

'Pol?' Meg's voice is shaking. 'Pol, it's me, Meg.'

'I know who it is.'

'I just... I just wanted to say sorry. I'm so very sorry. What I said last night, it was really out of order. I don't know why I said it.'

There's silence on the other end of the phone.

'I'd had too much to drink,' Meg carries on. 'I went a bit mad, because I haven't been away on my own for such a long time. Not that it's any excuse, but I drank far too much and I was so pissed I wasn't thinking straight. I wasn't thinking at all.'

There's another long silence; Meg can only hear her own heart beating. 'Pol?' she whispers, eventually. 'Are you still there?'

'Yes, I'm fucking here, Meg. To be honest, though, I don't know what to say to you.'

'No, I can understand that. You must hate me.'

'Close.'

'Oh God, I'm so sorry.' Meg is crying now, her breath coming in jags, her forehead resting on her hand as she bends over the phone.

'Did you really not realise what you were saying?' Polly's voice has risen. 'Did you not think about the effect that might have on me? On my wedding? On my bloody marriage?'

'I didn't mean to say it out loud,' sobs Meg.

'Oh, well that's alright then! You only thought it. You only thought that my husband was sleeping with one of my best mates. Not only sleeping with her – getting her pregnant! But you only thought it and didn't intend to say it out loud, so that makes it all fine!'

'No! I don't mean that. I just...' Meg has no idea what she means. Nothing she can say will make this any better.

'You were wrong, you know.' Polly's voice is hard, clipped. 'What you said in the marquee last night was a load of crap.'

Meg nods, even though nobody is there to see. 'Yes, I realise that now. I misunderstood something, got the wrong idea. It would never have happened if I hadn't been drinking. But I shouldn't have said it.'

'No, you shouldn't. But you did, and it has caused me a lot of pain, Meg. Adam and I are fine – no thanks to you – and I know what you said isn't true, it's just something you cooked up in your sad little head. But you could have ruined my marriage – my bloody one-day-old marriage! You almost managed to ruin the wedding day, although to be honest we had a fantastic time right up until the end, so your little scene last night won't be the thing we remember about all this.'

'Good,' whispers Meg. 'I'm glad.'

There's another silence, stretching on for seconds that feel like hours.

'In years to come, we might even laugh about it,' says Polly, calmer now. 'Though I can't imagine that yet. You could have done so much damage, Meg.'

'I'm glad I didn't.'

'Me too.'

'I'm sorry about your dress too, I got blood all over your beautiful dress. Please let me pay for it, get it cleaned for you. I'll buy you a new one.'

'Don't be ridiculous. It's just a dress.'

There's a sound in the background somewhere, a door closing near Polly, a male voice. She starts talking to someone, her voice muffled and unintelligible, as if she's put her hand over the microphone.

'Listen, Meg, I can't talk anymore. We're leaving for the airport soon and I've got some stuff to sort out.'

'Yes, of course. I didn't know if you'd answer, I thought you might not take my call. I'm so glad you're okay, you and Adam. I've been really stupid. I couldn't bear it if...'

'Let's leave it there, Meg.'

'Right, yes of course. Thanks for speaking to me.'

'I've got to go.'

'I'm so sorry again, and I love you.'

'Bye, Meg.'

She sits on the bed, not bothering to wipe away the tears that drip down her cheeks. She has no idea whether she will see Polly again after this weekend. It seems unlikely. Her friend will probably decide there's no room in her life for the person who almost single-handedly wrecked her wedding day and, if that's the case, Meg wouldn't blame her. Even if Polly does get in touch at some stage, it will be awkward. And how will she face Adam? He must hate her guts. Although, Polly hadn't got round to introducing Meg to her fiancé before now, so there's no reason why she should make any effort to get them together after all this.

She pushes herself up from the bed and goes into the ensuite. She must shower and try to make herself presentable before she goes downstairs. Was she right about Adam and Nancy? God knows, but it's immaterial. Polly believes her new husband when he says there was nothing going on between him and her best friend. She believes him when he tells her he's not the father of Nancy's baby. She needs to believe him for the sake of her future. Whether or not there was any truth in what Meg said, doesn't matter now.

Twenty minutes later, she has finally stopped crying and is wrapped in a towel after her shower. She sits on the bed to make the other important call. Pressing Joe's name on the screen, she holds the phone to her ear, her hand trembling as she hears it connect and start ringing. She clears her throat and takes a deep breath; she must put on her brightest voice to make sure she doesn't sound as massively hungover as she feels.

The phone rings and rings and eventually the voicemail clicks in. Meg is relieved and doesn't leave a message, tapping out a text instead:

> Tried to call, but no reply! Just going for breakfast, will call again in a bit xx

It will be better if she speaks to Joe once she has eaten and had some coffee. She's feeling so shitty that she doesn't trust herself to sound as upbeat and positive as she will need to sound, while she lies to her husband and says she has had the most amazing time with all her oldest, special friends in this classy Welsh hotel, where her poky attic bedroom has cost them an arm and a leg. Despite everything that has happened over the last twenty-four hours, she must pretend that Polly's wedding has been fun and fabulous, rather than a total shit show.

CHAPTER TWENTY-TWO

This morning all the tables have been put back into the marquee and laid up for breakfast. The place is busy and noisy and Meg hesitates at the entrance. She ought to be looking for Ali or Nancy, but doesn't want to see either of them.

She feels slightly better than she did when she woke up. The shower helped, and she has taken four paracetamol, which is too many, but she was desperate. She's wearing jeans and a shirt and has washed her hair and scrubbed her face until there's no trace of the make-up which had caked itself onto her skin overnight. She thinks she looks okay – even if she feels so ill that she can't imagine ever being properly human again.

But as she scans the room, another memory from last night floods back: she was yelling at an old man, and it turned out to be not just any old man, but Polly's grandfather. Then she pictures the expression on Polly's mother's face, the care and concern which had so rapidly turned to disgust and disbelief. Meg cringes and blushes so intensely it feels as if sweat is about to pop out all across her forehead. How did that whole thing get so out of hand? If only she'd known who the man was. What he did was wrong – Meg is still angry about it and thinks she has a right to be – but she should have handled it better. And undoubtedly would have done, had she been sober. What will Polly say if she finds out?

But Polly has other things on her mind. Like the fact that Meg accused her new husband of fathering her best friend's baby. 'Shit,' she whispers, dropping her face into her hands. She steps back from the doorway. She cannot go into this marquee right now. Even if she doesn't bump into a member of Polly or Adam's family, there will be plenty of other people in there who witnessed her drunken rant.

'Morning.'

Meg lifts her head; Susie is standing beside her. Her face is so pale, her skin looks almost yellow. She smiles, but it's clearly an effort to do so.

'Susie, you look awful.'

'Cheers. You don't look so good yourself.'

Meg turns back towards the crowded marquee. 'I don't think I can face going in here.'

'Me neither,' says Susie. 'There's a coffee machine in the bar. Shall we try that?'

'Yes, please.'

From a scene of devastation last night, the bar has been miraculously restored to its former glory. The carpets are clean, the tables have been polished and rows of gleaming glasses are lined up on the shelves beside the optics. A coffee machine and cups and saucers are on a table to one side, and Meg presses the button to dispense two large cappuccinos. There's a basket of individually wrapped shortbread biscuits beside the coffee machine, and she grabs a handful of them, as well as several sachets of sugar.

Susie has collapsed into a bucket seat at a small table by the window. As Meg puts the coffee in front of her, she groans. 'I don't think I can even cope with that, just yet. I can't remember the last time I felt so rough.'

'Same here.' Meg shakes the sugar sachet before adding it to her coffee, then pours in a second one. 'I haven't had a hangover like this in years. I don't drink much nowadays, because of the kids. You know, early mornings and disrupted sleep.'

Susie makes a face. 'Sounds hellish. I'm not ready for all that yet. Which is just as well, since there isn't anyone on the scene who's potential husband material.'

'I thought you said at the church, yesterday, that you were seeing someone?'

'Yes, I am. Well, sort of. He's a nice guy, but I don't think we've got a future together. It's fine though, I'm not desperate to find someone at the moment.'

Meg can hardly remember what it was like to be dating. There was the on/off boyfriend Ed in her first year at Leeds, then before she started going out with Joe, she had a couple of one-night stands. One of which, of course, was with Luke.

In a rush, she remembers his eyes, slightly unfocused, and the way he leant towards her in the bar. She remembers the smell of his breath, the dryness of his lips and the way his hands had worked their way down her back to where her figure-hugging dress was stretched tautly across her bottom. And she also remembers how the thrill of kissing a man other than Joe, had made her loins tingle with pleasure and sent blood pumping furiously around her body. They were standing just a few feet away from here, over by the bar. What the hell had she been thinking?

She glances up at Susie, who's unwrapping one of the shortbread biscuits. Meg is pretty sure she saw them kissing, but maybe she was too drunk to take it in? She definitely saw what happened later, the scene inside the marquee. It was Susie who'd grabbed her arm and pulled her away. It was Susie who helped her stumble out into the night, then half-carried her back upstairs to her room.

'Thank you,' she says. 'For last night. For helping me. I really appreciate it.'

Susie looks up at her and smiles. 'That's fine. We don't have to talk about any of that, if you don't want to. It all seemed pretty stressful.'

'It was. I don't really know how it happened. Things just blew up. I need to go and find the others and apologise. If they'll even speak to me, that is.'

'Why wouldn't they speak to you?'

Meg sighs. 'Ali shared something with me, late last night when we were outside, and then Nancy was winding me up and I got so angry with her that I sort of told her what Ali had said. Then, as if that wasn't bad enough, I followed her inside and found Polly and she got covered in blood.'

'I saw that,' Susie says. 'I was dancing near her when it happened. Where did it come from? That was all very weird.'

'My feet,' says Meg.

'Your *feet*?'

'Yes, my shoes didn't fit properly and my feet were bleeding. Anyway, that was one thing, but what's really awful is what I said after that.'

Susie nodded. 'I heard.'

'Oh God.' Meg sinks back in her chair. 'I should never have blurted it out like that. I don't know why? I didn't mean to – the words came into my mind and I said them out loud. It was so bloody stupid.'

'Well.' Susie looks down at her coffee, stirring the froth with a teaspoon. 'We've all done stupid things when we're drunk. But for what it's worth, I don't think many other people heard what you said. It was so noisy in there and Polly's mum was getting all hysterical, thinking she was bleeding. There was a lot going on.'

'Maybe,' says Meg. 'I hope so.' She isn't sure that's the case though.

'Also, I don't think it was all your fault. Your friend Nancy is a prize bitch.'

Meg laughs in surprise.

'It's true! She was so rude to you earlier, when we were in the bar, treating you like a child and patronising you. It seems like a strange friendship, you and her. You're such different people.'

Meg is so surprised she can't think what to say. It has never occurred to her how her relationship with Nancy might be seen by someone on the outside. 'You're right,' she says, eventually. 'We're very different. But that doesn't mean you can't be friends with someone who isn't like you?'

Susie shrugs. 'Of course not. But it helps if that person actually *likes* you! Sorry if that sounds brutal, but Nancy doesn't seem to have much time for you.' She unwraps another shortbread biscuit and dunks it in her coffee. 'So,' she pauses. 'I had no idea Nancy was pregnant – it must be early days because she doesn't look it. I hope you don't mind me asking, but do you really think that's true – about her and Adam?'

Meg sits back in her seat and shrugs. 'I don't know, Susie. No, is the answer. Or maybe. I really have no idea. It all seemed to make sense last night. They were strange with each other, earlier in the afternoon at the reception, and then she told me and Ali she was pregnant, but that the baby's father wasn't the boyfriend she's been with for a while. It sounds ridiculous, but it was just the way she and Adam were behaving when they were near each other, and then that look he gave her, later. I was sure there was something going on.'

'You may be right,' Susie says. 'But the big question is, what's going to happen now? Poor Polly, what a shitty way to end her wedding day. Do you think she and Adam will be okay?'

Meg nods. 'I think so. I called her earlier, to apologise. She told me he's denied it and she believes him.'

'Of course she does,' says Susie. 'She has to.'

'I wish I could take it all back.'

'Well, that's the one thing you can't do. But don't beat yourself up too much. It will all work itself out. Somehow. If there is something going on between Adam and Nancy, maybe it's better Polly finds out now, rather than further down the line?'

'She says there isn't. They've obviously talked it all through and he says it's not true.'

They sit in silence for a minute, sipping at their coffees. Meg suddenly realises there's something she wants to share with this woman. She has only just met her, they've had one drunken evening together, yet she feels closer to her than to any of the other people at this wedding. 'Susie. Can I talk to you about something?'

She needs to tell Susie what happened at the party. This huge, festering secret has been hanging over her for the last few weeks, while she lied to everyone about it and hoped nobody would ever find out what she'd done. She'd started to believe the secret was safe, because she was the only one who knew what had happened. Well, almost. Two small boys also knew, but neither of them was telling.

The birthday party had been nearly over. With the help of half a dozen other parents, Julia and Dave had got through three hours of noisy chaos. Barney, the birthday boy, had been as charming and funny as he always was, and the sound Meg remembers hearing above all else that afternoon was his high-pitched shriek of a laugh.

On that special Saturday, he was five years old and the star of the show, and he was loving every second of it. The magician brought him up in front of the other children and miraculously conjured up a selection of soft toys which he seemed to pull out of Barney's ears; he won the second game of pass-the-parcel (with a little help from his dad, who was doing the music); he threw himself on and off the bouncy castle that had been set up in the car park; he ate a huge birthday tea and his little face lit up with joy when his mother brought out a cake in the shape of a big red digger, five fountain candles fizzing on the top.

Ollie had been in a strange mood all afternoon and, at one point, he had pushed Barney over on the bouncy castle. Barney hadn't been hurt, but Meg had grabbed Ollie by the hand and pulled him away, using the excuse that one of his socks had almost fallen off. 'I'm watching you,' she'd whispered to her son, as she knelt beside him to one side of the huge inflatable, tugging the sock back over his ankle. 'Don't mess around today, do you hear me?'

With only twenty minutes until the party was due to end, Julia had put on some music at the end of the hall. Most of the children and their parents were dancing under a hastily erected mirror ball, when Meg saw Barney and Ollie running into the kitchen. She wound her way across the hall, past the groups of jumping, screeching children. As she pushed open the heavy fire door, she saw the two boys over by the fridge in the corner.

When she walked in and the door slammed shut behind her, Ollie turned and Meg saw he was holding a knife. She gasped and stopped, her heart racing, her brain trying to understand what was in front of her. Barney was pushing himself back against the wall and his eyes were wide with shock, his mouth open to let out a scream that was still stuck inside his throat.

'Ollie!' Meg could hardly hear her own voice over the sound of the music outside. 'Jesus Christ, Ollie! Put that down.' She started to move forward and then things happened very quickly. Her son turned his back to her again and she saw a flash as he pulled back his arm. The blade was several inches long and his fingers were clasped so tightly around the handle that his knuckles had turned white.

Then Barney lunged forward and Ollie was screaming out in pain, the knife clattering to the floor. As Meg reached them, Barney's teeth were sunk into the skin of Ollie's forearm and the two of them were collapsing in a tangle of limbs, their heads banging together, their little bodies thumping against the wall and onto the lino.

'Let go!' Meg had yelled, grabbing Barney and dragging him away until his jaw opened again and he slumped back against the fridge, the skin on his little face shockingly pale against the blood smeared across his front teeth and lips. There was more blood pouring down Ollie's arm and her son's screams turned to wails as he held it across his body.

When she looks back on that moment, Meg has no idea what made her hide the knife. It wasn't as if she thought any of it through – she barely had time to register what was happening – but she knelt down and picked up the knife from the floor, before pulling open a cupboard beside her and throwing it into the very back of the bottom shelf, behind piles of plates and bowls, then slamming the door shut again.

The boys weren't watching her; Ollie was crying and holding his arm, Barney was still crouching against the fridge, staring at his friend, his expression one of pure terror.

Meg wanted to grab her little boy and pull him to her, hug him and tell him everything was going to be fine: his arm would stop hurting, the wound was only skin deep and would heal, everything would be alright. But she also wanted to shake him so hard his teeth would rattle. She wanted to force him to look her in the face and acknowledge her. She wanted to scream at him until he told her why he'd been threatening his friend with a knife. She wanted to make him realise that none of it was okay; this time he'd gone too far.

And then the kitchen door crashed open behind her and Dave's voice broke across the blare of the music. 'What's going on in here? I heard screaming?' And Meg was struggling to her feet and grabbing both boys by the hand, pulling them towards him. 'Thank God you're here, Dave. These two have got themselves into a bit of a state.'

As she tells Susie about it all now, she feels surprisingly calm. When she finishes, they sit in silence for a few seconds, watching a woman carry a tray of clean cups across to the coffee machine and begin to stack them on the table. Meg knows Susie is looking at her, but keeps staring down at her hands in her lap.

'Why did you lie about it?' Susie asks, gently.

It's a fair question and even now – weeks later – Meg hasn't got an answer. 'I didn't plan to.' Her voice is so low, it's almost a whisper. 'When we went out into the hall, everyone rushed over and all the other parents and kids were gathering around Barney and Ollie – a couple of them started crying because both boys were covered in blood. It looked so much worse than it actually was. It was chaotic and all the parents were talking and wanting to know what was going on. Julia came up and asked what had happened, and I just answered her question.'

Sitting here in this elegant hotel bar, she can still picture the expression on Julia's face; horror rapidly replaced by confusion as she stared down at her son, his lips and teeth still smeared with the bright red blood of his best friend.

'Barney?' Julia had asked. But the little boy hadn't said a word. He just stood in silence, surrounded by his classmates and their parents. Afterwards, Meg realised he was probably in shock. He didn't say anything to defend himself because he didn't really understand what had happened.

'Why would he do that?' Dave had asked.

'This isn't like him at all,' one parent said.

'He's not that kind of child!' added another.

Maybe Meg imagined it, but she sensed an unspoken suggestion that, although this wasn't like Barney, it wouldn't have surprised anyone if the child to do the biting, had been her own son.

Ollie had history: he had bullied, fought and victimised his way through the first few months in Reception. He was already known as a bad boy: the one who had hit other kids, stolen their snacks at breaktime, thrown paint at them in art lessons, hidden their favourite toys.

Meg had grown used to getting emails from the head and being called over by Miss Carmody at the end of the day to be told what new drama her little boy had caused. She already knew he would get the blame whenever anything went wrong – not just now, but throughout his time at school and beyond. At just five years old, he had got himself a reputation which would be hard to throw off, and what hurt Meg most of all was that she knew it was a reputation he deserved. She loved her son so much: he was her firstborn, her special boy. But he was also a little shit.

'It didn't seem fair,' she says to Susie, now. 'I knew everyone would assume Ollie started it and that they'd say it was all his fault. I just wanted to protect him.'

'But he did start it?'

'I know. At the time it didn't feel like a lie, I just didn't tell them what had been going on before. I said I'd walked in and seen Barney biting Ollie. I missed out the bit about the knife.'

'But the other parents – particularly Barney's parents – they must have asked the boys what happened?' says Susie. 'To find out why they were fighting?'

Meg nods. 'Of course they did. Everyone was talking at once, trying to calm Ollie down, wiping the blood off his arm.' Meg remembers Julia kneeling in front of Barney, shaking him gently to get a reaction from him. 'Why did you do it, sweetheart?' she'd asked. 'What were you angry about?'

Then Barney had taken a huge gulp of air, his eyes focusing on his mother's face in front of him and he'd burst into tears, great heaving sobs twice as loud as the wails that were still coming from Ollie. 'I don't know!' he cried. 'I don't know.'

'I was waiting for him to mention the knife,' Meg says to Susie. 'I couldn't understand why he wasn't defending himself and telling them what Ollie had done. But he didn't say a word. It was almost as if the shock of the biting, overshadowed everything else. Poor Barney. I know he did it in self-defence, but he's such a lovely little boy – I doubt he'd ever been involved in something as scary as that before. How many five-year-olds have had a knife pointed at them?'

'But you could have told everyone else what really happened,' Susie says.

'Yes,' nods Meg. 'I could have told them. But I didn't. I know it's wrong. I know Ollie was out of control and he got away with doing something appalling. I also know this isn't the first time and he's got serious issues we need to address. I tried to talk to him about it, later that evening when we were back home, but he wouldn't even meet my eye. He didn't react, it was like I was speaking a foreign language. He turned away and looked at the wall.'

Susie leans forward and puts her hand on Meg's arm. 'Meg, he really needs to see someone. He needs some help.'

Meg nods. 'I know.'

'What's your husband's take on it all?'

There's a long pause. Meg studies the empty coffee cup on the table in front of her, rubbing her finger around the rim. When she finally looks up, Susie is staring at her expectantly.

'Joe doesn't know.'

'What?'

'He knows Ollie and Barney were fighting, but he doesn't know what I did. He thinks Barney started it...'

'Meg, this must have been so awful for you, keeping this all to yourself and trying to deal with it.' Susie gets up from her chair and moves across to hug Meg, holding her tight for several seconds.

Tears gather in the corner of Meg's eyes. She doesn't deserve sympathy or kindness for any of this, yet she needs this hug so badly.

'He ought to know the truth,' Susie says, gently, moving back to her seat. 'Ollie is his responsibility as much as yours. You both need to deal with this.'

Meg nods. 'It's just been hard finding the right time. Because I didn't tell Joe the truth straight away, it has just got worse and worse, the longer it goes on. Every time I try to pluck up the courage to tell him, it feels even harder and I can't face it. But I *am* going to tell him. We need to do something about Ollie.'

CHAPTER TWENTY-THREE

M eg finally catches sight of Ali and Nancy sitting at a table over in the far corner, their heads bent towards each other, and she takes a deep breath before starting to walk through the room. She strides purposefully, holding her head high, waving to someone here, saying hello to someone else there, making it seem for all the world as if she's not feeling like her temples are about to explode and an alien with a whisk has taken up residence in the pit of her stomach.

'Hey Meg!' someone calls. 'Great night, wasn't it?'

She turns and sees Daniel leaning back in his chair at a table near the far wall. He reaches out and grabs her hand, pulling her towards him. 'I hear you were a bit of a sensation on the dance floor!' he's saying. 'How's your head this morning?'

Meg tries to smile and knows she ought to say something, but her voice is caught in her throat and she can't think about anything other than the fact that Luke is sitting in the chair beside his brother. He's facing away from them, talking to a man on the other side, gesticulating as he describes something. But even this partial view has given her such a shock, it's like she's been slapped.

She looks back at Daniel, who's waiting for an answer. 'I've felt better!' she laughs.

Part of her wants Luke to turn around and notice her, but a much bigger part wants to run away. How will he be feeling about what happened last night? Will he even remember it? This kind of thing probably happens all the time to Luke: kissing women he hardly knows, getting off with them at parties. He's a good-looking bloke and there will be no shortage of women willing to let him run his hands all over their bodies – even if they aren't as drunk as Meg was.

Then suddenly, he's turning round. 'Well, look who made it down to breakfast! How are *you* feeling this morning?'

She smiles at him brightly. 'Like shit, to be honest. But I can't complain because it's all my own fault.'

'Well, you weren't the only one putting it away last night,' says Luke. 'I managed to fall asleep fully dressed – can't remember the last time I did that.'

Meg has no intention of admitting she did the same.

'But it was great, wasn't it?' Luke continues. 'What a brilliant wedding. Trust those two to do it in style.'

He is behaving as if nothing happened between them last night. Maybe this is deliberate and he's embarrassed. Or maybe he really was so drunk he doesn't even remember kissing her in the bar? She can't decide which would be worse. She should let it go, but Meg can't help herself: she wants to get some sort of a reaction from him.

Daniel has turned away and is talking to the woman sitting beside him, so Meg moves round to stand behind Luke's chair. 'Um, last night. I guess we were a bit out of order?' She smiles, to show this is banter, she's not being serious.

Luke laughs. 'No, you weren't out of order at all, you were funny!' He stands up from the table. 'Anyway, I'm just on my way to get my third breakfast, this buffet is amazing. I may catch you before we head off, yes?'

She stares at him, not quite believing what she has just heard. 'I mean *we* were out of order,' she repeats. 'Not just me. You and me, Luke. Snogging in the bar like a pair of teenagers.'

He steps back and puts his hands up in front of him, as if to ward her off. 'Whoa. Get back in your box, Meg! It was just a kiss for fuck's sake. I didn't ask you to bloody marry me!' He barks with laughter, then looks confused when she doesn't react. 'I mean, are you serious? Is this a big deal or something?'

Meg frowns and shakes her head at him. 'Well, it wasn't nothing. It sounds like it wasn't a big deal for you, but I feel bad about it. I was drunk and I got carried away and I'm ashamed of myself.'

He rolls his eyes. 'Well, if you want absolution, then you can have it. I forgive you, Meg! Don't get yourself all worked up on my account. Listen, we had a few drinks, we kissed. End of story. Let's not turn it into a bloody drama.'

She stares up into his handsome face. What is she hoping to achieve? Luke is a serial flirt – he probably groped and kissed a couple of other women last night. For him, this sort of behaviour is par for the course, and he can't understand why it means anything to her. And actually, he has a point – why *is* she making a big deal out of it?

This is about her, Meg, trying to make herself feel less guilty. It's also about the fact that, despite being a happily married mother of two small children, she has carried a torch for this man for years now. She fell for him at Leeds, hook, line and bloody sinker, and has never quite got over him. More fool her. Sharing that drunken kiss with him last night was a good thing, because it has made her realise it's more than time for her to move on. He's good looking and fun and great company. But he's also a womanising shit, and he never felt anything for her. This one-sided love of hers has run its course.

She smiles up at him. 'Yes, you're right. Let's forget about it.'

Luke is shaking his head at her, his brow furrowed as if she has just asked him something extremely complicated. 'Jeez, get over yourself,' he mutters, as he turns away.

Meg watches him throw his napkin onto the table and head over towards the breakfast buffet. She'd love to run after him and kick him, but she's not in any state to run anywhere – and she has caused quite enough scenes for one weekend. Sod him.

'Lovely to sit next to you yesterday!' she says to Daniel, touching his shoulder to interrupt his conversation. 'I probably won't see you later, so have a good trip back.'

She takes a deep breath and walks towards the table at the far end of the room, where Ali and Nancy are sitting. They're deep in conversation. As she approaches, they look up at the same time and Meg sees similar expressions flash across their faces: surprise, followed by something colder.

'Hi,' she says, pulling out a chair.

Neither of them speak: Nancy glares at her, Ali looks down at her hands.

'Listen, I want to apologise.' Meg stares down at the table as she runs her finger across a crease in the white linen cloth in front of her. 'I have no idea why I got so pissed last night, but I behaved really badly. I'm not sure what got into me.'

She looks back up; she knows these two women so well that the smallest details on their faces are imprinted on her mind. She knows the little dimple on Ali's left cheek and the way her brow knots whenever she's concentrating on something. She knows the pattern of Nancy's ear piercings and the scar on her top lip, which she got when she fell off a swing as a child. For years she has thought she loves these two faces, in the same way that she loves Polly's face, and Joe's and Ollie's and Tallulah's.

'To be honest, quite a lot about last night is a bit hazy,' she continues. 'But I'm pretty sure I said some awful things. I was rude to you, Nancy, which wasn't fair because you were only trying to stop me behaving like a dick.' She looks across the table at Ali. 'And Al, you told me something in confidence and I have no idea what made me mention it afterwards. That was unforgiveable.'

Ali is still looking down at her hands, but she nods.

'I think...' Meg falters. She doesn't want to sound as if she's justifying herself. 'I was feeling insecure – like I always do when we're all together. That's not your fault, it's mine. I need to stop worrying what other people think of me, I know it's pathetic at my age. But I always feel like a bit of a loser when I'm with you. You're both really successful and talented and so in control of your lives – Polly as well – and I'm just... well, I'm not any of those things!'

Ali opens her mouth to say something, but Meg carries on. 'I'm not fishing, or saying this so you can disagree. It's a fact. I'm not pretending there's any excuse for getting pissed and being such an idiot either.'

Ali says, 'I'd be lying if I said I was feeling a hundred percent, right now. You're not the only one who overdid it last night.'

Meg smiles at her gratefully. It's not exactly forgiveness, but it's possibly more than she deserves.

The three of them sit in silence while a waiter swoops in to take away the empty plates in front of Nancy and Ali. Then another one sets a coffee pot and jug of milk in the centre of the table. Wisps of steam come from the spout of the pot, while all around them people talk and laugh, cutlery clanking against china.

Meg glances up at Nancy, who's ignoring the coffee pot and sipping from a glass of water. There are dozens of questions racing through her mind. With the evangelical fervour of a new mother, Meg wants to know physical details: when did Nancy first suspect she might be pregnant? How bad has the morning sickness been? Are her boobs so tender it makes her want to scream? She would normally love offering support to a pregnant friend, but even if this weekend hadn't gone so horribly wrong, Nancy isn't the sort of person to take advice from anyone, however well meant. It's immaterial anyway, because Meg is now the last person who'll be invited to visit when Nancy's holding that scrap of a new baby in her arms.

And what part will Adam play in it all? Probably none; he has clearly managed to persuade Polly he isn't the father of Nancy's baby. But when they were queuing up to greet the bride and groom, yesterday, Meg saw the expression change on Nancy's face. The smile she had for Polly, disappeared as instantly as if someone had flicked a switch to turn it off. She hadn't just greeted Adam more coolly; she barely greeted him at all. And he was the same. A couple of non-committal words, then they turned away from each other amongst the throng of guests reaching out to hug and kiss the happy couple.

Meg may be putting two and two together and making five, but the more she thinks about all this, the more convinced she is that she's right.

'Anyway, I guess that's it then.' Meg stares down at the table, lining up the silver cutlery on either side of the place setting in front of her, making sure the gap between the two forks is the same size as the gap between the knife and the spoon. 'I wanted to say sorry, and I've done that. The only other thing I need to tell you both, is that I think we've come to the end of our time, as friends I mean.' She looks up to find them staring at her. 'I've realised I don't need this anymore,' she continues. 'We had some good times at Leeds – we had some great times – and back then you were both an important part of my life. But things have changed – or maybe I've changed. Anyway, none of it feels the same now, and we're not really working, are we?'

Ali's eyebrows are raised and she seems about to say something, but Meg shakes her head at her. 'Don't pretend it's not true, Al. We've all grown apart over the last few years and, although that shouldn't matter with some friendships, it does matter with ours. This wedding has shown that. There are things I wanted to share with you both this weekend, stuff I wanted to unload about – my little boy... well, it doesn't matter now, but I needed some advice and someone to talk to. But it didn't feel as if either of you were there for me.'

Nancy tuts and lifts her glass to her lips. 'God, it really is all about you, isn't it Meg?'

Meg shakes her head. 'No, it isn't. But it's not all about you either, Nancy. I was really pleased for you when you told us about the baby, and–'

'Oh, you were pleased for me, were you?' Nancy slams her glass back down onto the table. 'You were so pleased for me, that your sad twisted little mind started working overtime and coming up with accusations about who the father was!'

'I didn't mean it as an accusation. It's just that you'd said you weren't still with Jeff and it wasn't his, and then it seemed like Adam was being weird with you...'

'It's none of your fucking business,' hisses Nancy, leaning forward across the table. 'You had no right to say what you did. Jesus Christ, what kind of fallout did you think that would create? How dare you? How fucking *dare* you?' Her cheeks are pink, and tiny spittles of saliva fall from her mouth onto the tablecloth.

'You're right. I shouldn't have said that out loud,' Meg says. 'I'm really sorry.'

'Too bloody right you shouldn't. You shouldn't have said

anything at all. You shouldn't have even thought it, because it's none of your business. Why don't you get that?'

'I do get that. You're right, it's nothing to do with me and I'm sorry for what I've done. I spoke to Polly earlier and apologised, but I have no idea how I can ever make it right.'

'You can't. End of.' Nancy is shaking her head and glaring at Meg as if she's a piece of dog shit on the bottom of her shoe. 'But I think I have a pretty good idea why you said what you did. It's because you want to ruin everyone else's life, because your own is so bloody sad!'

'That's the thing,' Meg says. 'My life isn't sad. It's not what any of you want to be doing, but I'm happy with my life and my choices. I love Joe, I love my kids. We haven't got much money and there are things we need to work through. But it's a good life.'

'Well, bully for you.' Nancy sits back in her chair. 'I hope you enjoy the rest of it.'

Meg nods. 'Okay, let's stop all this. I've had enough of it too. Thanks for the lift yesterday, Ali. I'll make my own way back to London.'

'Good,' snaps Nancy. 'I don't want to have to spend any more time with you.'

Ali doesn't say anything, but the expression on her face is cold.

There's a plate piled high with pastries in the centre of the table and Meg leans forward and picks up a pain au chocolat, together with a plain croissant. 'You're not going to be eating any of these, are you?' she asks the others. 'Hah! Stupid question. Just having to look at all these calories and carbs is probably turning those tiny stomachs of yours.'

She stands up, then reaches for an almond croissant as well. 'In for a penny.' Hugging them to her chest, she smiles at Nancy and Ali. 'Bye, girls.'

CHAPTER TWENTY-FOUR

B ack up in her room, Meg starts throwing things into her
suitcase. It's much emptier than it was yesterday because
she has tossed her grass-stained charity shop dress into the
wastepaper basket, has lost her cream cardigan and there's only
one blue stiletto lying on the carpet beside the bed, which is sad
because she really did love those shoes – even if they made the
most terrible bloody mess of her heels.

The M&S shaper knickers are on the floor of the ensuite
and Meg picks them up and chucks them into the wastepaper
basket as well. They are ridiculously tight and uncomfortable
and, even though she took them off hours ago, there are still
welts across her waist where the skin was pinched in for such a
long time. She will not be wearing them again, however much
they constrain her bulges.

She takes a bite out of the pain au chocolat and grins at
herself in the mirror. She spent all day yesterday trying to act
and look like someone she isn't, trying to compete with her stick-
thin peers who exist on protein bars and fizzy water and
consider chocolate biscuits to be the work of the devil. But

really, what's the point in all that? This is her; this is her body. Joe's right, she needs to love it for what it has been through.

Joe. She sinks down onto the bed. She is putting off calling him, not because she doesn't want to talk to him – she's desperate to hear his voice – but because so much time has now passed since that awful call last night and she's strangely nervous about speaking to him. She should have phoned him back straight away and apologised.

Hopefully he has forgiven her, because he reached out to her earlier, sending that conciliatory text pretending to be from Ollie, but she should have tried to call again before she went down to breakfast, instead of just sending a text in reply. The way she spoke to him last night was bad enough, but this morning she has even more to apologise for – not that she has any intention of telling him what happened with Luke. What possessed her to *do* that? She drops her head into her hands.

Despite what happened in the bar last night, Meg is not the unfaithful type. She hasn't so much as looked at another man since she and Joe have been together. She adores him; he's her best friend and her soul mate, the yin to her yang and all those other ridiculous clichés that people spout when they talk about relationships. However stupid they sound, they're also true: Joe is her everything. But last night, she pushed Joe to the far reaches of her mind as she wrapped her arms around Lovely Luke without the beard, and kissed him with a passion that probably surprised her even more than it did him. Just thinking about it now, makes her shudder. She would never have taken things further than that drunken kiss – however many vodka shots she'd put away – but before this weekend, she wouldn't have thought herself capable of even going that far.

Joe has been so sweet and supportive about her coming away this weekend for Polly's wedding; he was the one who insisted she go out and buy a new dress and book a room in this swanky hotel – neither of which they could really afford. By getting outrageously drunk and behaving so badly, she has let them both down. Her finger shakes as she picks up the phone and presses his number.

'Well, hello stranger!' There's a slight edge to his voice, a sense that he is holding back, not sure how she's going to be with him. But his voice is so familiar, it makes her eyes fill with tears. She has missed him.

'Hi,' she says. 'How are you?'

'We're fine. We're just at the park at the moment – thought I'd drag the kids out of the house while it was still dry.'

'Is the forecast bad for later?'

'The sun was out at first, but there's rain on the way.'

'Yes, it's not looking so good here, either. Heavy grey skies.'

Why are they talking about the bloody weather? She doesn't care if it's hailing stones the size of tennis balls outside. They both know they're playing for time, waiting to hear how the other one sounds, listening for tiny inflections in each other's voices, which will show how they're feeling and which way this conversation is going to go.

'What was the wedding like yesterday?'

'It was good, yes, really good. The hotel is fantastic, unbelievably luxurious, and the meal was amazing.'

'And how was Polly?' He's beginning to sound normal again, more relaxed.

'She was lovely – her dress was stunning, as you'd imagine – and she made this great speech at the reception. Typical Pol, feisty as always. Adam's mother clearly hated it, sat there looking like she wanted to scream.'

He laughs and she can finally hear warmth in his voice. She hopes hers sounds the same. Now that she's talking normally to her lovely Joe, the last twenty-four hours feel surreal, like a very bad, hugely embarrassing dream. Did she really do all of those things last night? Can she go home and pick up where she left off, pretending none of this happened?

'Have you taken loads of photographs?' he asks.

'Yes, I took a few.' Meg actually can't remember taking any pictures after they left the church. It's strange because that's usually the first thing she thinks of doing – her phone is always in her hand, ready to capture a special moment. Ali and Nancy probably have loads they could have shared with her on the drive back, but that's not an option now.

'Ollie!' Joe is holding the phone away from his ear. 'It's Mummy! Come and say hello!'

Then there's a scuffling sound and some rapid, childish heavy breathing and Tallulah's voice is in her ear. 'Mumma! It's Lula. Where you?'

Meg's heart feels as if it will burst out of her chest; the joy at hearing her daughter's voice is overpowering. 'Hello baby girl!' She asks questions that don't get proper answers, laughing as Tallulah chatters about the slide at the park and a dog they saw earlier with a very waggy tail. When Joe comes back on the phone, he's laughing as well. 'Honestly, this girl! She's such a livewire. She has had two breakfasts already this morning and still wants a biscuit now.'

'Joe, I'm so sorry.' Meg doesn't want to sour the mood, but needs to get the apology off her chest. It's sitting there like a lump of stone and she's finding it hard to concentrate on anything else. 'About last night, when you called me. I'd had quite a bit to drink.' This isn't the apology she needs to make, but it's the only one she can handle.

He laughs again. 'That much was obvious.'

'But those things I said, about wishing you hadn't disturbed me, when I was away on my own. I didn't mean them. I don't know why I was going on like that. It was the booze talking – God, I can't remember the last time I had that much champagne. Also, I think being with everyone again, so many people I hadn't seen for years, it reminded me of Leeds and the things we used to do back then. I know this sounds ridiculous, but it sort of made me feel like I'd got very old and boring, that my life was so dull...'

She trails off, waiting for him to react, but he doesn't say anything.

'I don't mean that – my life is *not* dull. Sorry, that sounded awful. But being here on my own, away from you and the kids, has been weird.'

Tallulah is singing in the background and it sounds like Joe is pushing her on the swing.

'Anyway, I just wanted you to know that I feel bad about the things I said. I love you so much, Joe. And I love our children and our life and I would never change any of it.' Her voice breaks, as she swallows down a sob.

'Hey! Don't cry.' He sounds concerned. 'Meggy, what's this all about? You got a bit drunk last night and you didn't want to talk to me while you were away with all your mates. That's fine! I understand. I must admit I was a bit pissed off afterwards, but only because the kids were being hard work and I was knackered. But it's not as if you go away very often – or at all. Afterwards, I felt bad for calling you – I should have left you to have a good time. You didn't need to be reminded about us while you were on a break. Seriously, this is not a big deal.'

She has messed up, but it's not something this lovely man of hers is going to make her feel bad about. Being Joe, he won't ever mention it again; she really doesn't deserve him.

'Listen, we'd better go,' he says. 'Ollie's in a bit of a bad mood this morning, and he's hiding in the bushes on the other side of the playground, so I need to go and make sure he's not torturing a squirrel or something!' Joe is laughing, but Meg catches her breath and squeezes her eyes shut at the mention of her son, suddenly remembering the injured little Jack Russell that limped away from him in the park the other week. She wishes now she'd pushed him harder about that, insisted on finding out what had happened. Torturing squirrels sounds about right.

Why didn't she tell Joe about some of the other things Ollie has been doing recently – not just the horrific incident at Barney's party, but the many smaller incidents which, like the pieces of a jigsaw slowly slotting into place, have started to create a larger picture in her mind? She can't start this conversation now, but she needs to address it.

'Text me later and let me know roughly what time you'll be back,' Joe's saying. 'We'll get a takeaway and open a bottle of wine tonight and you can tell me more about the wedding and who was there.'

'That sounds good,' she says, smiling though nobody can see her. 'Although I might pass on the wine.'

After ending the call, she stays sitting on the bed. Susie has offered her a lift back to Bristol, where she can get a train to London, but she won't be packed and waiting downstairs yet, so there's no rush. The housekeepers are clearly at work up here already: she can hear doors slamming and the rattle of trolleys being pushed along the corridor.

She scrolls through her social media accounts and then flicks through her most recent photos. She's right: she has seriously failed in that department. There are a couple of lovely shots of Polly and Adam standing together, talking to guests outside the church, but there are also half a dozen photos of the ground and Meg's own feet. She has never been the greatest photographer, but if she takes enough pictures she usually ends up with a few good ones amongst the rubbish. Not this weekend.

Scrolling back, she ignores all the recent photos she has

taken of her own children and eventually comes to the Saturday afternoon of the party. Barney's cute little face grins out at her, his wide smile beaming out from a face covered with chocolate cake and brightly coloured sprinkles.

It is such a huge relief to have told Susie about the party. During the last couple of weeks of term, she discussed what happened with some of the other parents, as they stood around outside the school gates having dropped off their children.

But those conversations were very different. All the other people who were avidly picking over the bones of what had happened, had also been involved: they were at the hall that afternoon – their offspring playing games, throwing themselves about on the bouncy castle and dancing under the mirrorball. They didn't know the truth about what had gone on in the kitchen, but they had witnessed the distressing scene afterwards and helped mop up the blood and comfort two hysterical little boys.

They had all believed Meg's version of events, because why wouldn't they? She was the adult. Even if Barney had been capable of explaining what had happened, there was no knife, no proof. Nobody would have believed a traumatised birthday boy, if his version of events had been put up against that of a sensible fellow parent.

She and Julia haven't spoken since. A few hours after the party, when Ollie's arm had been bathed and bandaged and he was tucked up in bed, Meg sent Julia a text. She agonised over the wording of it for ages, typing it out several times, then deleting it again. The message she eventually sent was short and friendly, asking how Barney was and thanking Julia for organising the party. She didn't mention what had happened and didn't mention Ollie. She kept checking her phone for the rest of the evening, hoping to see the three pulsating dots that would tell her Julia was writing a reply, but there was nothing.

Eventually, a message pinged in the following morning. Julia was apologetic, saying she didn't know what had come over Barney, and she hoped Ollie's arm was getting better. There was nothing overtly unfriendly about it, but there was also none of the warmth that had been in all the previous texts they'd exchanged since they first met outside the school gates when the boys started in Reception, four months ago.

Meg decided she was being over-sensitive and expecting too much: Julia had had a busy weekend organising the party, and a deeply distressing time when it ended, so she and Dave were probably exhausted – as well as confused and upset. It wasn't surprising they needed time to regroup and process what had happened.

Meg had picked up her phone and replied straight away, being a little too gushing:

> Please don't worry, let's forget all about it. That was such a lovely party, well done for all your hard work! Let's have a coffee next week? Xx

She never got a reply from Julia, and Barney wasn't at school for the first three days of the following week. The mums outside the gates talked about little else and, although she hated herself for it, Meg quite enjoyed being the centre of attention. But she was careful not to let that show. If anything, she pretended to be reluctant to discuss what had happened, and she wouldn't allow anyone to be critical of Barney, always defending him and coming out with platitudes: 'Boys will be boys!' 'They were just messing around.'

With her appalling secret tucked safely away, she needed to be the good guy in all this. It wasn't hard to ensure that happened; however badly her own son occasionally behaved, none of the other parents ever doubted Meg was anything other than sweet and kind.

By the end of that week, the incident had become old news. Barney came quietly back to school, Ollie stopped wearing his bandage as a mark of honour and life pretty much returned to normal. Meg tried to catch Julia at morning drop-off, but she always seemed to be in a hurry and, after a couple of brush-offs, Meg took the hint. She was pretty sure Julia knew there was more to it all than they'd been told, but why would Meg lie? Shortly after that, it was the end of term and, with Christmas coming up, Meg hoped everyone would forget about the party. It was such a relief not to have to stand outside those school gates for a couple of weeks.

Sitting here now, on the unmade hotel bed, she scrolls through her contacts until she finds Julia's name. Ironically, it's directly below Joe's. Her finger itches to dial it, to hear the voice of this woman she'd only recently got to know, but whom she had grown to like a great deal and had hoped would become a long-term friend. But there is no point in calling. Julia cannot forgive Ollie – and therefore she cannot forgive his mother. Meg understands that. She can't forgive Ollie either.

CHAPTER TWENTY-FIVE

The hotel reception is packed – it looks as if all one hundred wedding guests have decided to check out at exactly the same time and two harried receptionists are printing off invoices and running up and down behind the desk holding beeping card machines. Meg paid in advance, so only needs to hand in her keys, but Susie admits she attacked the contents of the minibar late last night, when she got back to her room. 'Crisps and a bar of chocolate,' she says. 'I was starving. Sorry, I'll have to join this queue.'

Meg goes to wait outside, but comes to a halt when she sees Ali standing to one side of the hotel steps. For a second, she thinks Ali hasn't noticed her, but then she glances up. It's too late for Meg to go back inside, and it would be ridiculous anyway. She needs to have this conversation. She wheels her case across and takes a deep breath. 'Hi, again. You okay?'

Ali looks at her coldly. 'Of course. Why wouldn't I be?'

'No reason. I wasn't suggesting anything. I just meant...' Meg isn't sure how to phrase this. She can't stop thinking about what Ali told her last night and, although she guesses her friend won't want to talk about it, she can't help wanting to dig a little deeper.

The more she thinks about it, the more confused she feels about what she learnt. At first, she was shocked – no, shocked is too strong a word for it. She was taken aback, that's for sure; not that Ali and Polly had briefly been lovers – that was the part that didn't really surprise her – but at the fact that the whole thing had passed her by. They'd been two of her best friends; how come she had no idea about it at the time?

If she's honest, she feels slightly put out. There's no reason why they would have told her what had happened, but why didn't she see any signs or pick up on any changes in their behaviour towards each other? It was one night of passion, but it sounds as if it was unexpected for both of them, so it must have had some sort of knock-on effect on the way they reacted to each other and behaved afterwards? But all that is irrelevant now, because Meg has blurted out Ali's hard-kept secret and she knows things between them will never be the same.

She takes a deep breath. 'I'm so sorry, Ali, about what I said last night. About telling Nancy about you and Polly. It was unforgivable. I was so drunk, but that's no excuse.'

Ali's finger freezes momentarily, above the screen of her phone, then a second later she continues tapping out her text. She doesn't say anything, or even look up.

'I honestly don't know why I did it,' Meg continues. 'It was none of my business and I completely understand why you're so angry with me. It was just such a surprise – not that it happened, but that you managed to keep it so quiet.' She is gabbling now, unsettled by the fact that she's getting nothing back from Ali. 'I'm not saying you should have told any of us about what happened, but it must have been hard – especially for you.'

'You've already apologised, Meg. Let's leave it, shall we?'

'I just feel bad that you didn't think you could trust me enough to tell me. Or Nancy. Or anyone else.'

'Nancy already knew.' Ali still hasn't looked up from her phone.

'Oh!' Meg is blindsided. She can't think what to say. 'But... How did she know?'

What she wants to say is, *Why did you tell Nancy but keep me in the dark? Why did you feel you could go to her and talk about this major event in your life, but not to me?*

But she can't say that, because it makes her sound jealous and insecure and needy. And the trouble is, Meg knows she is all of those things. Right now, she is asking questions about Ali's personal business because she feels aggrieved at not having been told all the details years ago, when they were at Leeds. She isn't now trying to find out more because she's concerned about how Ali has lived with her big secret or coped with being the victim of unrequited love for such a long time. Her motivations are purely selfish.

Finally, Ali stops texting and looks back up at her. Meg suddenly feels as exposed as if she was standing outside this hotel stark naked. Her cheeks are burning and she's aware Ali can see straight through her.

'Nancy knows what happened, because Polly told her, after we left uni, when they were travelling together in South America,' Ali says. 'I didn't know that at the time, and I was a bit pissed off when I found out, because I wouldn't have wanted it to get spread around and become common knowledge. But it was only Nancy she told, not the entire student population of Leeds. And we'd left by then anyway. So, it wasn't such a big deal – Polly had every right to tell her. I could have talked about it as well, if I'd wanted to.'

'But you didn't want to,' Meg whispers.

'Not particularly. It was different for me; that night with Polly was important to me, but – as I told you last night – I knew from the outset that it meant very little to her. So, I had no right to ask her to keep quiet about it. All I could do, was hold my head up high and pretend it was one of those things, when Nancy brought it up, a long time afterwards. We had a laugh about it. Or rather, I pretended to laugh about it.'

'Oh, Ali,' Meg says. 'How horrible.'

Ali shrugs. 'That's just how it was.'

'Well, I'm still sorry you didn't feel you could tell me about it. I wish I could have been more supportive.'

'I'm getting over it, Meg. I know I was a bit of a mess last night. But that was mostly alcohol talking – too much booze always makes me maudlin. Don't worry, I haven't been sitting around pining over Polly for the last few years. I've had other relationships – while we were at Leeds and more recently. I haven't turned into some kind of grieving nun.'

Meg isn't sure she believes her; she has never met any of these other people who Ali is claiming have figured in her life, and last night it sounded as if she didn't feel she would ever get over what happened. But Meg can't say that. She also can't ask any more questions – not about the timing, or about how Polly and Ali's relationship changed afterwards, or whether they've ever spoken about it since. She is desperate to know all these things, but Ali clearly wants the subject closed; she is looking back down at her phone and scrolling.

It's impressive Ali managed to put on such a brave face over the last twenty-four hours, despite hating this wedding and everything it stood for.

This morning she seems so composed, totally in control, and that's the version of herself she likes to present to the world. The weeping, distraught Ali who admitted her ongoing love for

Polly, was definitely an aberration and not one she wants anyone else to see.

Meg can understand why she'll want to pretend those emotional moments and full disclosure never happened, and she and Ali are unlikely to stay in touch after this. Seeing Meg would remind Ali of her own moment of weakness.

'Right, well I'll leave you to it then,' Meg says. 'Thanks for the lift up here.'

She can't stand around outside any longer with Ali ignoring her, so she grabs the handle of her suitcase and wheels it back into the reception area, stopping to wait just inside the door. This all feels so strange. Just twenty-four hours ago, she was sitting in Ali's Audi, reminiscing about their shared past, believing she was off to have a fun time away with her three dearest friends.

Now, they've had the most hideous falling out, none of them are speaking to her and their friendship is over. Ali and Nancy will get back into the car again shortly and set off for London without her. They will have hours to go over it all, and pick apart the wedding, the row, the revelations – as well as the part Meg played in it. They will undoubtedly pick apart her life as well: her insecurity, her weakness, her inability to hold her drink, and the fucking mess she has created.

But as she stands here, in this beautiful Welsh hotel, Meg realises she doesn't actually care. There is still a tiny bit of hurt lurking inside her – she has shared history with these women and you can't just write off something like that without consequence. But what's happened over the last twenty-four hours has made Meg realise so much about herself and her so-called friends.

Even when they started their journey outside Hammersmith tube yesterday, she was not as close to Ali and Nancy as she'd been telling herself. She was the outsider all those years ago, back in Leeds, and she is still the outsider now. It's about time she learnt to accept that and get over it. Strangely, the realisation doesn't upset her as much as she would have expected.

She sighs and turns around to face the reception desk again, just as somebody stumbles against her case.

'Oh, I'm sorry!' Meg is dragging it out of the way, when she looks up and finds herself staring at Polly's mother. The woman's eyes widen slightly as she realises who's in front of her.

Meg wants to say something, but as images flash through her mind, she can't find any words. She remembers Polly's mother grabbing her by the arm and pulling her up from the dancefloor; she remembers a glass of water being pushed towards her; she remembers the kindness on the older woman's face. And, of course, she remembers how it all went so suddenly and unpleasantly wrong.

She glances swiftly over Polly's mother's shoulder, subconsciously looking, she realises, to see if the old man is with her. He is nowhere to be seen, but blood is pounding in her ears as her eyes flicker back again. Part of her is disappointed, because she still itches to get another chance to glare at him and point out the wrongfulness of what he did. But she's mostly relieved, because she also knows she has said and done more than enough to offend this family. For an instant, she thinks everything will be fine: that Polly's mother won't remember who she is. But as the woman widens her eyes, the expression on her face settles itself into angular hardness and her cornflower blue eyes are steely as they bore into Meg.

'Good morning!' Susie is suddenly beside her, leaning forward. 'How are you, Mrs Johnson? Thank you so much for such a fabulous day yesterday. You gave Polly and Adam such a wonderful send off.'

The woman's gaze shifts sideways and, as she looks at Susie, the muscles in her cheeks relax slightly. 'Thank you,' she says. 'I'm so glad you enjoyed it.'

'Oh, we really did. This is such a fantastic venue.' Susie has moved so far forward that she has almost pushed Meg out of the way, and suddenly Meg realises why. She is overwhelmingly grateful and steps back towards the bar, shrinking away from the conversation and the conflict.

'Are you going straight home, or do you have other plans for today?' Susie continues. 'I hear Polly and Adam are flying to Morocco. Lucky them – I'm very envious, I've always wanted to go there and if they're lucky it will be quite warm. Did Adam arrange it as a surprise?'

Another woman with bright red hair is standing behind Polly's mother and she glances at Meg and raises one eyebrow. Who the hell is this? Meg feels she ought to know her, or at least understand there's a connection somewhere. The woman's face is familiar, so they may well have spoken last night. If she's with Polly's mother, she's family or a close friend, which means it's also likely she either witnessed the scene at the table in the marquee or the one later, in the middle of the dancefloor. Both catastrophic incidents caused by Meg, which Susie is now determinedly trying to steer them away from.

'Lovely to see you!' Polly's mother's voice is now warm and she has her hand on Susie's arm, as if they're the best of friends. 'Take care driving home.'

'And you!' Susie says. She has moved so far round, she's completely blocking Meg from view. Meg wants to hug her.

Then Polly's mother is turning away and other people are milling about them, and Susie has averted the potential awkwardness. As she lets out the breath she didn't know she was holding in, Meg hears a voice in her ear. She turns to find the woman with red hair leaning towards her, so close she can see the tiny pore-sized indentations in the face powder which has been blotted across her cheeks.

'Well done,' the woman whispers. 'Her father has always been a randy old goat – we all know it. I heard what you said last night; good for you, for calling him out.'

Meg's eyes widen and her mouth drops open in surprise. In less than a second, the women has winked at her, turned and moved away.

CHAPTER TWENTY-SIX

The rain starts before they reach Newport, and within minutes the windscreen wipers are on their fastest setting, snapping furiously back and forth, clearing the splatters of water only briefly before they flood across the glass again.

'Thank God it wasn't like this yesterday,' Meg says.

'That would have been awful,' agrees Susie. She has a tiny little Fiat 500 and is a careful, slightly nervous driver, hunched forward over the steering wheel, wearing a pair of huge round glasses that keep sliding down her nose.

Since they left the hotel, a couple of hours ago, they've chatted endlessly about the wedding – how beautiful Polly looked, how lovely the church service was and how the hotel was the ultimate in luxury, from the set-up in the marquee to the accommodation. They laughed as they remembered that bit in the best man's speech about Adam getting stuck in a hotel lift in Amsterdam with a strippergram; then laughed even more at the way his mother's face turned puce and she looked as if she was being forced to suck on lemons, clearly hating every minute of her son's special day.

They've also talked about themselves. It turns out that Susie is a dental nurse, working at a large practice in Bedminster in the south of Bristol. She grins when Meg says she can't think of anything worse than spending all day staring into people's mouths. 'No one believes me, but I love my job! My brother's a chiropodist – now that's a really disgusting thing to do for a living – all those crusty corns and manky toenails.' They both scream in mock horror at the thought, then laugh again. They've done a lot of laughing on this drive – so much more than Meg did when she was sitting in the rear seat of Ali's Audi yesterday morning.

Susie has also asked about Meg's life – gentle questions that have allowed her to talk about how she often feels out of her depth nowadays. Once she started talking, she found it hard to stop.

It was the conversation she wanted to have yesterday, with Nancy and Ali, but now she's glad that didn't happen. Listening to what she did at Barney's party, they would have thought she was an over-protective, obsessive mother, who would go to any lengths to defend her child, whatever the cost to someone else. They would have been right.

But Susie seems to understand. Or even if she can't fully understand, she listens, which is all Meg needs right now. Most important, she isn't judging, which is allowing Meg to admit she has known for a while that Ollie isn't just clumsy and exuberant, he's a difficult child – however hard it is to be honest about that.

'Joe's a great believer in talking things through as a family,' she says, as the little Fiat drives across the bridge spanning the vast grey expanse of the River Severn. 'He thinks Ollie is old enough to understand the difference between right and wrong, so if we explain why he shouldn't be doing something, he'll eventually learn how to control himself.'

'But you don't agree?'

'Not anymore. I used to think that was the way to deal with him – it feels as if it should be. When you go online, it's what's recommended by all the child-rearing experts. But Ollie isn't the sort of boy who responds to that approach. The trouble is, I don't know what he will respond to. The only other option we've come up with is punishment, but that doesn't make much difference either. A couple of months ago, he hit Tallulah so hard with the TV remote that one of her front teeth came loose, so we got angry with him and said we were going to ban him from watching television for a week. But he wasn't bothered, he just shrugged. He wouldn't apologise to Tallulah either.'

Susie signals to take the turning off the motorway towards Bristol, grasping the steering wheel so hard that her knuckles turn white. Meg stops talking so she can concentrate, and stares out of the side window at the wet grass verge.

While Joe describes Ollie as 'an individual', Meg knows there's more to it than that. The Reception teacher, Miss Carmody, has mentioned ADHD and Joe's mother, Anne – with her usual lack of tact and diplomacy – has bandied around terms like autism and personality disorder.

But so far it has been easier for them to dismiss concerns and insist their little boy is just settling into school. This is a phase, they tell each other: his behaviour isn't great at the moment, but he will come out the other side as a more settled, rounded, confident child. Meg thinks Joe really believes that and, by not telling him about every little incident that has happened at school – as well as Ollie's unpleasant behaviour away from it – she has enabled her husband to naively continue to think there's nothing wrong, and his son is just high spirited.

For a long time, she has known she should have been more honest with Joe, but she has kept so much hidden from him, that she doesn't know where to start. The secrets and lies about their son's out-of-control behaviour have piled up and the whole thing now feels so far out of her control, it's like waiting for a tsunami to crash down upon them all. But just talking to Susie during this journey, has made that tsunami seem a little less terrifying.

A vast lorry overtakes the tiny car, throwing up so much spray they're temporarily and terrifyingly blinded, when the windscreen wipers working at full pelt can't clear the screen quickly enough. 'Bloody hell!' Susie says, huddling even closer to the steering wheel. 'This is not my idea of fun.'

'Thanks for taking me with you,' Meg says. 'I don't know how I would have got back otherwise.'

'I'm sure someone would have given you a lift,' Susie says. 'And I'm only getting you halfway home!'

'Maybe, but I've enjoyed being with you.'

Susie turns briefly and grins at her. 'Me too. It's been great to meet you, Meg. A real bonus from this weekend. I have to admit, I wasn't looking forward to the wedding. It's hard going to these things on your own, not knowing anyone. Thanks for letting me latch onto you.'

'Right back at you,' says Meg. 'You've been a lifesaver.'

CHAPTER TWENTY-SEVEN

Susie pulls up outside Temple Meads railway station. It's Saturday afternoon and the place is heaving. A group of middle-aged men in football shirts are coming out of the main entrance, and some teenage boys are straggling along the pavement, their matching red lanyards and the frantic signalling of an adult tour leader, suggesting they're in Bristol on some sort of exchange. They saunter past, talking too loudly and jostling against the car door as Meg tries to open it.

Susie helps Meg lift her case out of the boot, and they smile and hug tightly, as if they've known each other for years. 'I'll text you when I'm next coming up to London, shall I? We can get together for a coffee or a glass of wine?'

'That would be great,' says Meg. 'Make sure you do. Thanks for everything.'

Susie steps away and starts walking back to the driver's side. 'And good luck telling Joe,' she calls. 'You're doing the right thing.'

Meg nods, then waves energetically while the Fiat pulls away and heads towards the exit. As it disappears into the traffic, a bus pulls up in front of Meg, blocking her view.

Passengers begin to jump off and a man knocks against her case and glares at her, so she grabs it and wheels it into the station. Her phone pings and she knows it will be a reply from Joe. She texted a few minutes ago, to say she'll be back a bit later than planned, hopefully by late afternoon:

> Getting a train from Bristol, long story, will explain when I get home xx

She has only been away for just over a day, but can't wait to see them again: Joe and Tallulah. It hurts to admit it, but she isn't looking forward to seeing Ollie. She loves her little boy, but is beginning to let herself acknowledge that she doesn't like him very much at the moment.

As she stands on the platform, waiting for the train that will take her back up to Paddington, she rehearses how she's going to start the conversation with Joe. She's dreading it already, and feels slightly sick.

She has no idea how he'll react to what she's going to say, but she needs to put things right. She has to tell him what happened at Barney's party. She has never kept anything from him before – especially not something this big – and the fact that there is a secret she shares with her five-year-old son, but not with her husband, feels awful.

Joe has always been principled. Meg knows he'll be shocked when he hears what actually went on in the kitchen of that hall, and he'll be appalled at what she did afterwards, and a little ashamed. Perhaps she isn't quite the person he has always thought she is. But, however he reacts, it's important she owns up to her part in this.

Will he really be surprised to hear about the knife? Possibly not. Just because he has a tendency to excuse Ollie's bad behaviour, doesn't mean he's blind to his son's failings. Thanks to Meg's lack of candour, he may not have been aware of every little crisis over the last year or so, but there have been enough incidents to make him stop and think. There's a chance that deep down he will have been as worried as she has been. If Meg can start the conversation and suggest that Ollie needs help, she knows Joe will want to do the right thing.

An announcement blares out from a speaker, directly above Meg's head: 'The train shortly arriving at platform four is the 13.30 Great Western Railways service to London Paddington, calling at...'

So, tonight, over the takeaway and that bottle of wine – which she still doesn't think she can face drinking – she will tell Joe about the knife and what Ollie was about to do to Barney.

Together they will then speak to Ollie about what really happened. Meg is expecting they'll get little from him – she remembers the coldness in his eyes as he stared at her, that night after the party, seeming to look straight through her, before turning away and facing the wall.

Whatever happens though, they will start the process of getting Ollie some help, finding someone who can work out what's going on in that little head of his. She isn't sure who that will be – a child psychologist presumably – but there will inevitably be doctor's appointments and referrals, interviews and tests. She surprises herself by how calmly she thinks about all these things. What they're about to embark on won't be easy, but it's essential.

The train arrives in a thundering rush of air and hissing brakes and Meg heaves her case into a carriage, rolling it down the aisle ahead of her until she finds an empty seat.

She must also go to find Julia and apologise, owning up about what happened. This is the thing that terrifies her the most. Joe loves his wife and son: even if he's shocked, he will ultimately be supportive. But there's no knowing how Julia will react. She has the right to be very angry.

When Meg has dropped Tallulah at nursery on Monday morning, she will track down Julia. Although her former friend was avoiding her at the school gates before Christmas, Meg is familiar enough with her routine to know she works from home at the start of the week, so she will go to Julia's house and ask if they can talk. She isn't yet sure what she'll say, or how she'll admit to her own part in what happened – it would all be so much easier if she could understand it herself. But the bottom line is, she covered up for Ollie and pushed the blame onto Barney, and that must be put right.

Julia needs to be reassured that her child is the kind, caring, sensitive little boy she always believed him to be, not the hysterical monster who took a chunk out of a fellow pupil's arm and now refuses to talk about what happened.

The train journey to Paddington is quick and stress-free. Meg rests her forehead against the window and dozes for most of it, her exhausted and hungover body lulled by the rocking and clattering as they speed towards London. At the other end, she fights her way through crowds heading for the Underground. It hardly seems possible that just a few hours ago she was in the middle of rural Wales, away from all this noise and dirt and commotion.

When she finally emerges back into the daylight at East Finchley tube station, she stands on the pavement for a few seconds, taking in deep gulps of fresh air, not caring that it's drizzling and that she doesn't have a hood on her coat. Despite everything that happened over the last twenty-four hours, and the awful way she behaved, Meg feels strangely light. It's not physical, it's a different sort of lightness. For the last couple of weeks, this horrid business about Ollie and the party has been like a rock, stuck in the pit of her stomach, and now she can finally see a way in which to dislodge it.

This peculiar lightness is also in part due to the events of the last twenty-four hours. She has fallen out so badly with her three friends, it's inevitable she won't be seeing them again. Yesterday morning, that possibility would have left her bereft, but right now she feels calm about it. There is some residual hurt left deep inside her, and some sadness – they did share some great times – but overall, what happened at that luxurious hotel in Wales was for the best.

Home is a short walk away and she can feel the pull of it as strongly as if there's a rope attached to her waist which will tug her along the High Road, then down the fourth turning on the right, then left at the T-junction.

As she sets off along the road, pulling her suitcase behind her, she suddenly remembers Polly and Adam's wedding present. When Nancy put Ali on the spot yesterday, in front of the happy couple, Ali said she would forward it, but Meg has no idea how she'll manage that – it will cost her a fortune. Having said that, Ali can easily afford to get it couriered across London, and she did admit it was her fault the horrendously expensive coffee machine didn't make it to the wedding with them. Maybe she'll drop it round to Polly's when they get back from their honeymoon.

Either way, it's not Meg's problem and, for once, she doesn't bother working out a way in which she can get involved in the delivery of the belated wedding gift. Ali is perfectly capable of sorting it out and, even if she needed some help, Meg would now be the last person she'd go to.

Turning right into a side road, she adjusts the waistband of her jeans, which is rubbing uncomfortably against her skin. Serves her right for spending the last twenty-four hours eating and drinking as if it was going out of fashion. She'll have put on a couple of pounds, but so what. Now her stomach has settled and her headache is receding, she's feeling upbeat about everything – even her own body. Especially her own body! As she strides down the road, she makes a resolution to stop beating herself up about the size of her hips and the saggy skin on her belly.

If she cared about it that much, she would stop snacking on the biscuits she claims to buy for the children, but eats herself. If she cared about it that much, she would stop hoovering up the leftovers from the kids' plates at tea and standing in front of the open fridge picking at cold sausages and sticking her finger into tubs of houmous. If she cared about it that much, she would stop eating entire bars of Dairy Milk while Joe is out playing squash, then hiding the empty wrappers down the back of the sofa when she hears his key in the lock.

'There are worse things than being fat,' she says out loud to herself. She knows she is privileged and has a good life and a husband who loves her. She needs to overcome this inherent insecurity which has stalked her for the last few years and accept herself for who and what she is.

After all, if she can hold her head high after getting paralytic at the wedding of one of her closest friends, insulting the grandfather of the bride, unzipping her dress on the dancefloor, throwing up in the bushes, getting blood all over the bride and accusing the groom of fathering a child with one of his new wife's best friends, she can find the resilience within herself to face up to whatever else in her life needs to be addressed.

At the T-junction at the top of the road a Tesco delivery van is reversing around the corner, its warning beepers blasting urgently as the driver negotiates the parked cars on either side. Meg steps back, waiting for it to get past and, as she does so, her phone pings. She pulls it out of her back pocket, expecting to see a text from Joe, asking where she is, or from Susie, checking she's home safely.

But it isn't a text, it's a Facebook notification. Although she uses Instagram, she isn't very active on Facebook and rarely posts but she quite enjoys lurking on there and seeing what other people are getting up to. A photo appears: it's Polly and Adam, standing on the steps outside the church, yesterday. They're turned towards each other, laughing, and crowds of friends and family are gathered behind them, waiting to pour out of the church and make their way down the path. Meg holds the phone screen closer, knowing she was at the back there somewhere, but there are too many faces and she can't see herself.

The photo has been put up by Catherine Weaver; she was in the debating society with Polly at Leeds and Meg saw her at the wedding, although they didn't speak. Meg had forgotten they were friends on Facebook, but they must be, otherwise she wouldn't be seeing this.

Catherine has added an overly sentimental message with lots of emojis, saying how special it was to be part of Adam and Polly's big day. This first picture is one of dozens. As the van continues to reverse, Meg flicks through them. They're beautiful! Here's Polly getting into the carriage, and Adam hugging Connie, the bridesmaid. Here's the reception, with close-up shots of the immaculately laid tables and those pretty miniature roses. What happened to all of those? Maybe the guests were meant to take them home with them.

She flicks on again: the speeches – including a lovely close-up of Polly as she made hers – the wedding cake. Oh, these are wonderful. It won't matter that she didn't take many photographs herself, because she'll be able to show all of these to Joe later. Then there are pictures of the evening: the waiters serving more champagne, the band in the marquee, people drinking and talking. And... oh fuck... the blood drains from Meg's face as she realises what she's looking at.

The last photo on this post was taken in the hotel bar. A woman in the foreground is grinning at whoever's taking the picture, holding up her glass in a toast. But behind her, a couple are locked in an embrace. The woman's back is to the camera and the man's hand is on her backside. You can see half of the man's face and it's obvious they're kissing. The woman looks like she's about to topple over and is virtually hanging off him, her arms around his neck. She's wearing a dress, which from this angle looks a little too tight; it's cream, with a pattern of blue and purple flowers on it.

The van has finished reversing and now shunts into gear and moves away again, going back the way it came. As it roars past her, the driver sticks up his hand, thanking her for waiting. Meg is looking straight at him, but doesn't see him. Her heart is thundering in her chest and her hand holding the phone is shaking. By the time she looks back down, it has timed out and the screen is blank. She taps it and swipes urgently to get back to the Facebook post. The photo pops up again. Meg tries to enlarge it but, because the couple are in the background, the detail grows fuzzy.

She feels sick.

The kiss meant nothing; Luke meant nothing. Or maybe for a while there, she thought he meant something – although God knows what. But at breakfast, he'd been so arrogant and dismissive, and his rudeness was a good thing because it helped her finally realise she'd been spending too much time thinking about someone in her past who wasn't worth the effort. Meg had loved him once, but should have moved on long ago. What their drunken kiss confirmed was that Luke isn't worthy of her time and attention and it has also shown her that she can forget about him. Since she walked away from him this morning, she has been planning to lock up that stupid moment of drunken madness in an imaginary box in the far reaches of her mind and throw away the key.

But now it's here for everyone to see. On Catherine Weaver's Facebook page, with its settings on *public*.

There's a low wall beside Meg, and she collapses onto it, still unable to take her eyes from the photo. She scrolls back through some of the previous pictures, then forward again to this one. She brings the phone closer to her face and tries to enlarge the image. Again, it grows too fuzzy.

How many other people are going to see this? Even if they do, will they know it's her in the photo? In all likelihood, the answer is no. A handful of guests at the wedding might recognise this very blurry photograph of her rear view, but only the ones who know her well enough to remember what she was wearing. And, ironically, Meg won't be staying in touch with any of them. The only person she'll be in contact with who might see this and know what happened, is her new friend, Susie, and, although they didn't discuss it, Meg is pretty sure Susie witnessed her drunken clinch with Luke anyway.

There's only one other person who might see this who matters, and that's Joe. If he comes across this photo, he may recognise the dress that she twirled around in so proudly, after finding it in that charity shop the other week. He might also recognise the back of her head, although her hair is dishevelled and it isn't curling down over her shoulders in the way it usually does.

But the thing is, Joe isn't on Facebook; so, there's no reason why he should see this photograph.

She stands up and reaches for the handle of her case, walking slowly up to the T-junction where she will need to turn left. She can see her house up ahead on the other side of the road: her happy place.

For a moment, she considers calling Susie, and asking for her advice. But there's no point; Meg knows what she has to do.

And she also knows that, whatever happens, this new friend of hers will be there to support her.

Just twenty-four hours ago, as Ali drove her towards Wales, Meg thought she knew everything about her friends; they were so close, they were aware of each other's secrets and could call out each other's lies. It turns out that isn't the case; not only were those particular friends not the best, but they're pretty good at hiding things. Meg isn't in any position to judge: she has been good at hiding things too. But it's time for all that to stop.

Before she saw this post, she'd already decided to come clean with Joe about Ollie, and she's still going to do that. She's also going to be honest about this wedding and explain what a bloody nightmare it has been, and how badly she behaved. She's going to tell Joe everything she did – from vodka shots and throwing up in the bushes, to her drunken half-undressed dancing and the way she managed to insult the groom, the bride and her extended family.

It isn't – as Luke suggested – that she wants absolution. It's just time she stopped hiding things.

She has reached the house, and stands outside it for a moment, looking at the peeling paintwork on the front door, the muddy children's wellies kicked off on the doormat. There's a big pot to one side, in which she planted a wisteria last summer, hoping it would grow up the wall and eventually drape itself across the top of the door frame. But it didn't get watered properly and now there's just a withered brown husk left in the pot. She should have dug it out months ago but somehow stopped noticing it. She will tackle that tomorrow; it will be a day full of fresh starts.

She opens the gate and pulls her suitcase up towards the front door. Even if there's no chance of Joe ever seeing the Facebook post, Meg is also going to tell him that she shared a brief drunken kiss with a man she had a crush on, years ago, back in Leeds. God knows how she'll tell him this, but she will find a way. If she's going to fully unload about her behaviour this weekend, she needs to include all the sordid details. Just because a secret is safe, doesn't mean it should remain a secret. She may need that glass of wine, after all.

She can't be bothered to find her keys, so lifts up one hand and knocks on the door. From somewhere inside the house, she hears Tallulah's cry of excitement and through the glass panel in the door she can make out the shape of her little girl running down the hall towards her. She can't stop smiling and her heart feels as if it's about to burst through her chest. Life is good; she's a lucky woman.

It's a shame about that blue stiletto though...

THE END

ACKNOWLEDGEMENTS

There are always so many people to thank when a book finally sees the light of day. As usual, I'm grateful to the wonderful Bloodhound team for all their ongoing hard work – Betsy, Fred, Tara, Hannah, Lexi, Rachel – and a particularly big thank you to Clare Law, my amazing editor, who does such a great job of making sure everything hangs together and reads well. She is a delight to work with and I trust her judgement implicitly, so when she likes a book, I breathe a huge sigh of relief! She liked this one, so I hope readers will agree.

The other person who needs a special thank you is Liza Bewick, who read a very early version of this book for me and is always so supportive of everything I do. It's the best feeling in the world when good friends like her have your back. And finally, the Clan: Mat, Sam, Maddy and Jessie, you constantly inspire me and fill me with love and enthusiasm for life.

If you'd like to find out more about me or my writing, you can follow me on Facebook Sarah Edghill Author or on Instagram @sarah.edghill

A NOTE FROM THE PUBLISHER

Thank you for reading this book. If you enjoyed it please do consider leaving a review on Amazon to help others find it too.

We hate typos. All of our books have been rigorously edited and proofread, but sometimes mistakes do slip through. If you have spotted a typo, please do let us know and we can get it amended within hours.

info@bloodhoundbooks.com

Printed in Great Britain
by Amazon

58471791R00128